Advance Praise

FROM THE AUTHOR of the recently released *In Search of the Body Immortal: Let the Journey Begin* and other popular publications, readers experience another uniquely spun story to readers; where Dystopian meets Spiritual in an astonishing mastery of imagination.

In multiple interlocking, parallel worlds Dr. Robert J. Newton's popular characters, James and Ann are looking for answers to myriad mysteries of life, spirituality, a world torn by too much government control. The unusual abilities James has to communicate with his deceased wife, Ann, is the key to intertwining a fascinating plot of one man's quest to return the world to it's most natural state; a people shedding the constraints of an unwanted government and seeking to return to the natural ways the Creator intended.

Newton's writing is inventive and tests the boundaries of storytelling. *The Planet of the Stupids* reveals the lives of animals being lived out in a parallel manner with humans on Earth, where both civilizations are clinging to life... living in the left-overs of a government out of control. The reader is prepared to find the answers to several vital questions:

Will the parallel worlds, where fear reigns supreme, be just the beginning of the end, or is there a way to turn the tide and battle against political and religious domination?

Does Newton use the parallel worlds to express his own fears about the current world in which we live?

Is he stepping courageously forward, taking a stand for a world currently wrought with more shady dealings and instability that we are aware?

Is there merit to the similarities the author provides··· showing the animals the stupidity of humans who are slowly being swallowed by a monstrous bureaucracy and government secrets from which no one can ultimately escape?

Planet of the Stupids may well be a wake-up call; a welcome to the world of dystopia... a world of government and societies going in a horribly wrong direction. Does James, as the messenger, bring home the reality of what transpires when civilization invades and dictates virtually every element of our lives? The author uses fascinating twists and James' unique capacity for observing what transpires—across multi-planets—when a government wields its power against its citizenry and creates an elitist state. Do the animal kingdoms on these parallel universes fight the system—or are they doomed—forever being ground to dust by the blackened boots of tyranny?

Famine, war, pestilence; in the biblical sense, these would quite possibly be seen as the end of the world. In Newton's dystopian tale, with a flare of paranormal, we see a chilling collection of added elements... of biological warfare, ecological disaster, cosmological tragedy, and a government's covert efforts of total exploitation, i.e. human control.

As usual, Newton's remarkable book has myriad facets; it is so rich in content that introducing is it not an easy task. The material is unique; most of his knowledge has been gleaned from resources not readily available to the average reader. Newton has studied from the guardians of knowledge the world over. This is not the first time Newton has shared his depot of knowledge; nor I venture to guess, will it be the last. We are just fortunate to have access to the awakening it provides.

The topics introduced in each of Dr. Newton's books can well be considered explosive! They reveal possibilities of the transformations possible for an earth ran amuck. Even if you are not sure whether you see Newton's work as anything other than fiction, you should certainly consider the possibilities of the psychic and extrasensory powers of which he writes. Certainly not an eloquent argument for a more complete reality in which a fifth, spiritual dimension plays a core role, Newton creatively takes into account recent events – including 9/11 and the war in Iraq—and addresses myriad timeless issues, from the validity of his own religious experiences. *Planet of the Stupids*, akin to Newton's other stories, has an amazing capacity to open one's heart and mind to reconsider personal spiritual growth, and that of business, relationships, and daily life.

Through the creative use of fiction, Newton causes the reader to pause and consider how God factors into our beliefs. Very subtly, the author asks you to consider old theories, now discarded as you read a thrilling journey into the mysteries of multidimensional space, and the possibilities parallel universes do indeed, lay somewhere closely aside our own.

~T. R. Stearns, EdS, Retired Superintendent of Schools,
Editor

Planet of the Stupids

*Bringing Back the Light of God
to Planet Earth—With a Paradise Found*

Planet of the Stupids

*Bringing Back the Light of God
to Planet Earth—With a Paradise Found*

By

Robert J. Newton, J.D., N.D

Beyond the Bounds of Earth Publishing, Entertainment and Education

ISBN-13: 978-0996137157

ISBN-10: 0996137157

Dr. Robert J. Newton

Great Motivational Talks
Beyond the Bounds of Earth Publishing,
Entertainment and Education

20253 Evening Breeze Dr.
Walnut, California 91789

http://www.drrobertnewton.com/

Ordering Information:
Quantity sales. Special discounts are available on quantity purchases by corporations, associations, and others. For details, contact the publisher at the address above.

Printed in the United States of America

First Edition

14 13 12 11 10 / 10 9 8 7 6 5 4 3 2 1

Dedication

THIS BOOK IS dedicated to you if you are someone who:

Has such an intense thirst to know and understand God you will overcome any obstacle put in the path of your pursuit.

Always question everything; yet remain pliable enough to accept new information that might be contrary to what you have already learned.

Do not necessarily understand something when it is presented to you, but wisely suspend judgment until you can ascertain the accuracy thereof.

Is never reticent to ask for scientific and annotated proof of what someone presented to you, especially those who ask you to accept something on blind belief. I am referring to religions that promote you believe their teachings with no questioning of their validity!

Knows as certitude you can accomplish anything when you put your thoughts, energy, and powers of visualization toward accomplishing your goal.

Lives by the maxim, "The fool didn't know it couldn't be done, so he went ahead and did it anyway."

Can embrace the reality that many novels are written in such a manner as to entertain the reader, whilst planting new seeds of thought and ground breaking information.

Table of Contents

Acknowledgements

A **WRITER IS** only as good as his sources, his personal connection to other worldly sources such as the Akashic Records, and his imagination and creativity! Herein, I choose to acknowledge the personal sources, each of who helped me to finish a more complete book.

Charlette Ann Smith, deceased, was my wife of thirty-seven years and was my main source and inspiration that brought this book to fruition. Her knowledge of Kriya Kundalini Yoga, Hinduism and Sanskrit mantras was unparalleled on planet Earth and she constantly gave me information and inspiration in my writings.

Cindy Cardenas shared with Charlette and me the Dr. Paul Foster Case Builders of the Adytum (BOTA) information, including *The Emerald Tablets of Hermes Trismegustis*, Dr. Case's *The Pattern on the Trestle Board* and *The 72 Names of God*, from Exodus, in *The Torah*.

Dr. Paul Foster Case was a Renaissance Man, and infused with much esoteric and alchemical knowledge and one of his books is *The Spiritual Keys of Alchemy*. Whenever you go into the land of creating an immortal body, it is helpful if you do so in the context of alchemy. The organization he created—Builders of the Adytum (BOTA) still dispenses his teachings.

Yogi Marshall Govindan Satchidananda initiated me into the highest levels of Kriya Kundalini Yoga. Kriya

Kundalini Yoga has directly enhanced my awareness of the increased light factor in my body, and my ability to channel the creative process and solve problems.

Bertha Eloina Nash has helped me manage my day-to-day affairs. Possibly too often she is a "writers widow." She is a shining example of living from the Heart.

Prologue

WHEN I WAS a teenager—was it back in a time when dinosaurs roamed the Earth—I had to read a most amazing book in high school, George Orwell's *Animal Farm*. As much as I loved the story, I never believed the things Orwell wrote about would come to fruition... on planet Earth... in the United States of America. Maybe that is because I did not want to believe such things could be true! Yet, Aldous Huxley's *Brave New World*, and other amazing books I read, likewise validated Orwell's book.

Many people feel doomed to be controlled by socialist, totalitarian governments. Indeed, we may already be in this predicament! My tale is about how this happened, but even more so, about how we transcend the shackles of Communist, socialistic governments, who fervently believe government is more capable of directing our lives than we are! Most people today are completely oblivious just how insidious the tentacles of Socialism are. Little by little, it creeps in and advances upon us, until we have lost all freedom and liberty!

I will contend that those who believe otherwise have not kept their eye on the ball and are in danger of being struck out by the pitcher in a figurative baseball game. The caveat here is you need to be ready for the curveball because a lot of them are being thrown our way. Historically, not being able to be ahead of the curveball has kept many a good player out of the major leagues, including possibly the best basketball player of all time, Michael Jordan.

There's a certain glaring irony of socialist and Communist governments: their main purpose in life is to pass laws to *de facto* extort money from us and to control and subjugate us, but the very people who pass the laws restraining our liberty and freedom are the ones least capable of following their own laws. There are no known exceptions to this statement! Such behavior is known as co-dependency, which is the need to control others, when they are actually incapable of controlling themselves! It is vastly easier to control someone else rather than confront our own shortcomings! So it could be said any Socialistic or Communist government is based upon co-dependency, an inherent personality defect and dysfunction, to wit!

You might think this story would be easy to tell, yet for me it would have been easier to describe a scenario from the miasmas of hell. The American Revolution was predicated on creating a government free from the tyranny of the directives of monarchies, kings and queens and the nefarious banking system that comes with them. The *Federalist Papers* were essays written by various American founding fathers; a common theme in the collective articles was that people should be sovereign as to their governments. It meant the nation's people should hold a superior position and rights over their government. Only a few of the founding fathers, most notably, Alexander Hamilton, felt the government should be sovereign over its people, or as he referred to them... subjects! Please join me for a most incredible and revealing journey, with many twists and turns, into myriad miasmas and traumas therein and how animals on a parallel Earth avoided all this and lived lives of freedom and bliss!

Once again, James and Ann, my characters from *The Hidden Codes of God, Beyond the Mists of Time: When Trees Ruled the Earth,* and *In Search of the Body Immortal: Let the Journey Begin,* use their powers of remote viewing—psychically going into the past and future—and revealing things very few people have considered casually, let alone seriously. What James and Ann encounter is something few people, other than quantum physicists, would ever consider.

As James transports himself back to a time beginning in 1959, meets Ann sometime after this, he finds three Earth's with subdivided and shared dimensions in a third dimension Earth and three subdivided parallel dimensions existing in the fourth and fifth dimensions. The complexity of this topic reveals some rewarding solutions to problems consistently encountered by everyone existing on third-dimension Earth. I hope you enjoy the possibilities of life and living we will encounter, as those possibilities hold the keys to creating a Heaven on Earth. After all we have been through with our inherently dysfunctional governments, **as a God given right... as a people, we most certainly deserve and are entitled to something better!**

Dr. Robert J. Newton, August 12, 2015

CHAPTER ONE

Begin the Beguine

—————— ⁘⋆⋆⋆⋆ ——————

JAMES, LOOKING AT how corrupt and repressive and totalitarian the United States government was becoming and probably already really was, under the pretense of being a democratic republic, decided to use his psychic ability of remote viewing, a method of viewing things in an altered state of consciousness, akin to lucid daydreaming, to see what might have happened or is happening in a parallel Earth dimension or even higher-dimensioned manifestations of planet Earth.

One thing James knew for sure, from the remote viewing sessions, which he experienced while researching the ancient civilizations in *Beyond the Mists of Time: When Trees Ruled the Earth,* in an early planet Earth, at least in some Earth dimensions, things were created within the parameters of Nature and Natural Law, manifested by the Creator, itself. Similar to the beauty and harmony ethereally expressed in the song, *Begin the Beguine*, a lilting and gently flowing song, that was representative of a state of cooperation on Earth. For many eons, animals, trees and plants lived in a state of equality, where no species was superior to or dominated by any other species. With this type of "operating system," there was no need for a governmental structure, since all resources were shared equally and there existed no hoarding or

1

monopolizing of land, water or food! There was no need for a constitution; a governmental body, a medical system with doctors, hospitals and drugs; nor a police or military force.

True, the larger and fiercer animals would eat the smaller and tamer ones, but this was never done with the intention of gluttony or killing just for sport as did the American Buffalo hunters! Also, there were no civil or inter-species wars! So unless you were one of the animals ultimately eaten as food, life was good...very, very good!

James especially noticed, after the arrival of humanity on Earth, the natural ways of the animal and plant kingdoms was changed in many detrimental ways, over time! The first extra terrestrial beings that came to Earth, were, by and large, respectful of Nature and viewed and treated it with a great benevolence! In the ancient civilizations of India and Lemuria (Mu), this immersion into Nature created flourishing cultures, such as for the animals previously described—no constitutions, no governments, no hoarding of resources or money, no hospitals or doctors, nor police forces and military forces—because once again, these things were not needed, hence redundant! This concept is discussed in detail in *Beyond the Mists of Time: When Trees Ruled the Earth* where there truly was a Heaven on Earth! There was a perfection, of sorts, that began at the atomic level of creation and worked upward and manifested into the human level, as per "Aleph Kaf Aleph," the seventh Name of God, from Exodus in the *Torah*, which means to create or restore things to their perfect state! And so it was for millions... perhaps billions of years.

So the initial example left by Earth's early inhabitants was nothing but good, just as the Creator intended and designed things—with a precision virtually unnoticed by humanity today. This was, of course, irrespective of the saga of Adam and Eve, since this vastly predated that event and time, unbeknownst to our populace at large and basically

2

ignored by the world's religions, anthropology and scientific disciplines!

This, then is the point in time, when James decided to take himself into a deep state of meditation—via the Kriya Kundalini Pranayam breath—and with an expanded sense of consciousness that allowed him to go back in time again and again. What James drifted into at first was rather surprising, as he saw an Earth that was subdivided between animals and humans... a parallel dimension within a parallel dimension. As bizarre as this was, he would later see something that defied logic yet most definitely seemed to exist, nevertheless.

James kind of looked at all of this in dismay as he viewed that somehow, some way... things had been skewed in the Animal Kingdom. Some attributed this to a Pig named Atom and his wife, Electron, who violated the laws of God for all animals to follow, which supposedly God had sent down from Heaven at the beginning of creation, similar to Adam and Eve in *The Torah*. This resulted in a "curse" from God that would extend to all progeny born after this violation of God's laws... an "original of sin" of sorts.

Others viewed things in the light there could be no original sin, since everything was perfect, as per "Aleph Kaf Aleph," the 7th Name of God, from *The 72 Names of God* from the book of Exodus in the same *Torah,* and it was simply a misunderstanding of God's laws of Nature—a powerful illusion of sorts—that distorted people's perception of God and reality and thus separated them from the ever present light and guidance from God. As James viewed this scenario he spoke aloud, "It would have been invaluable if these animals had the direction of the 72 Names of God, and in specific, Hey Resh Chet, which keeps us connected to the light/God since they would not have had to have been held hostage from the acts of their ancestors. Yet most humans do not know about this, so can the animals really be faulted for such, likewise?"

3

Regardless of natural law, James was about to see that all of a sudden the Pigs thought they were more than equal, being above and beyond all the other domesticated animals... even though they were not the largest of animals, they could muster a fierceness of sorts! This all transpired about 1959 and the Pigs seemed to have learned some superior attitude from the humans on the subdivided parallel Earth and their forlorn human ways, in how they strayed from the guidelines of Nature, including the sharing of resources equally! James said to himself, "This was probably due to a morphic resonance, a field of energy that can be transmitted and affect people, plants and animals, nearby and even in other dimensions, as per the research of Dr. Rupert Sheldrake and Ken Keyes *The Hundredth Monkey.*"

The events took the other animals by complete surprise, since their actions most certainly violated an intuitive and accepted understanding among all the animals, as things had always been from time immemorial... and so they thought would remain! James watched with concern, as in very short order, the Pigs, The Piggiest Party and their leader, Ledig, consolidated the position of control, naming their country, formerly known as Abuc, Pig Land, All the while they were selling their power grab as a boon for all the animals and promising that everyone would be taken care of, like never before! This was a brilliant move... a propaganda ploy, where the Pigs words were not in alignment with their actions, especially since the propaganda was repeated incessantly.

Over time the messages served to convince the other animals of a new reality, based on the subtle and perpetual brainwashing and James thought, *Wow this is eerily similar to what has happens on my Earth, yet these animals lived for millions of years, if not more, in a state of unfettered perfection and it kind of boggles the mind how anyone could have bought into these blatant lies!*

4

Anyway, within a very short period of time, there were shortages of food, except for the Pigs. When the other animals complained about this turn of events, pointing out there were never shortages of food before the Pigs big power play, President Ledig would respond, "First that simply is not true but don't worry about it anyway, because soon things will be so much better. We are just going through the process of creating a new and better system of living and are in the throes of transition and assimilation!" James, having heard such empty promises many times before on his third-dimension Human Earth, just laughed derisively.

As James ruminated all of this it struck him how hauntingly similar this was as to what happened when Fidel Castro invaded Cuba with Che Guevara, ousted President Bautista in 1959, and shortly thereafter formed a poorly operating Communist government that never delivered to the Proletariat, the common people, what it promised! Indeed, on some levels the Cuban communist government made sure all people had medical care and an education. But all this support came with many flaws, not to mention a repressive, totalitarian government that was obsessed with controlling its citizens, even at a *minute* level.

Although the Pigs did not overthrow the government, per se, their leader, Ledig, touted how much better would be the plight of the animals than before, but so very hollow was this promise, since the animals had previously lived in a paradise and had no need of medical care or a formal education. Their previous education came from observing Nature and the "natural laws" observable therein. James saw, however, these disingenuous statements allowed the Piggiest Party and the Pig Elites to consolidate their power through a document akin to *The Communist Manifesto*, known as *The Union of Animals (El Union de Animales)*. This Manifesto supposedly exposed what were described as The Capitalist Bourgeois Elitist's, who became unduly rich at the expense of the Proletariat through the hoarding and monopolizing of resources!

It stated: "All Animals are equal and should share equally in the bounty on Earth!"

This was great in theory, but the reality was... this is exactly how the animals previously existed and what they had experienced long before Ledig and the Pigs decided they were more than equal to the other animals! The reality that betrayed Ledig's assertion was that the Pigs enjoyed a disproportionate amount of food and became very fat, while the other animals got less food and became thinner and hungrier by the day!

Since Ledig and the Pigs were in control of the entire food chain, the rare food shortages that occurred at the beginning of the Pigs' reign became chronic shortages over time. Any animal that complained about the shortages was labeled as a terrorist and summarily imprisoned for their comments. These actions were exercised within a legal system that was precipitously established, where none had existed before. Worse than this, said legal system was based on Commercial/Admiralty Law that stripped the animals of their Natural Law rights. This system of Commercial Law was rife with petty infractions and loaded with fines that rendered it nothing less than oppressive and vastly onerous. This was all allowable under the *Animal Constitution,* and *The Bill of Animal Rights.* The abject ridiculousness of the entire situation was that the animals always intuitively knew every animal was actually equal with each other and never lived in fear of violating an "animal law" or having money extorted from them.

It remains to be understood, however, just how the Pigs sold this unneeded folly as a way to guarantee the rights of all animals. For James, this was the typical SOP of any large government. As James pondered this, he recalled in soliloquy,

*such assurances are always baseless and very deceiving, in
light of the contrary results for this, but it just goes to show
you how effective incessant PR and propaganda can achieve
and deceive!*

As bad as the inequality and food shortage issues were,
the animals were not charged for the food they previously ate
for free, yet their allotment was not enough to survive. It came
to be that food for the animals was supplemented by supplies,
procured via a black market and sold outside government
channels! The animals had to buy food illegally at inflated
prices just to keep from starving. So much for the socialist,
Communist utopian dream, which actually more resembled a
nightmare! James, observing the irony of this, questioned, "Is
this always the way it is with utopias, which are an imagined
perfection, as per Sir Thomas More's book, *Utopia?* This is
really a pipe dream, a fantasy, rather than something that can
actually be created or manifested. How cruel is the irony of
this?"

As James viewed more, an unrest developed within the
community of animals, exclusive of the Pigs, subsequently
followed by a nominal police force, staffed only by Pigs,
which ballooned into a huge force not long thereafter. The
civil liberties guaranteed by The Bill of Animal Rights were in
fact almost non-existent. It is believed this disparity transpired
because the Piggiest Legislature, LARD, which was controlled
entirely by the Pigs, passed *The Defense of the Homeland Act!*
Police were everywhere and ready to arrest anyone who had
the audacity to complain about their lack of food or criticize
the government for any other reason.

James saw, as he viewed things most discomforting to
him, the best actual comparison to what exists in Cuba, North
Korea, and China, today, where people are arrested for even
the most minor of infractions or dissent and criticisms of the
government! So while there has been a fusion with a free

market economy with a Communist/socialist system in Cuba in the last few years, there is still an onerous police state presence, with informers lurking on all corners, just waiting to report people who violate any and all laws that are strictly enforced by a dictatorship. The same things occur routinely in North Korea, which means there is very little crime; it also means artistic expressions and unfettered creativity and dissent is squelched.

Since its founding, North Korea has been powerfully ruled by the Kim family. Most currently headed by Kim Jong-un, the country is under a state-run socialist government many consider to be a Stalinist dictatorship. The family's dedication to a military-first policy has led the isolated, impoverished and often famine-stricken nation to pursue a nuclear weapons program, which has done little more than incur sanctions and worldwide condemnation

As James was familiar with the obsessive control under which such governments seek to enmesh their citizens, he wondered, *Does fear of the loss of control over the animals drive the Piggiest Legislature, LARD, to begin to charge the animals rent for the space they occupied?* You can probably imagine this went over with about as much popularity as cancelling the celebration of Christmas and Hanukkah, for Christians and Jews, especially since all animals had previously inhabited any and all areas they desired without any concern for having to pay a fee to do so. It should be pointed out that such rent did not include a shelter—just raw land. All of a sudden, land that was held in common for all the animals, was parceled, but still owned by the state of Pig Land

Any animal who did not pay their rent or protested about such, was imprisoned and often left in jail without even a trial, similar to the debtor's prisons on our Human Earth in the 1800's and before, where prisoners were left to rot in jail indefinitely. James, uttered out loud, "Geez Louise, I thought I was viewing 1959 and onward, but the presence of debtors prisons makes it seem like I am still in The Dark Ages! Am I missing something here? I think not! You can only abuse and maltreat people for just so long and then eventually they rebel! It always happens! For these animals, hopefully it is much sooner than much later!"

In a state of disbelief about what he was viewing, James continued his observation of the situation, more quietly... thinking, *I might just have to interfere with the space-time continuum, ignore the Prime Directive, and lead these animals out of their dire situation, if other help does not soon manifest itself for these animals! Not so oddly, I have the same scenario where I live in the United States; not a debtor's prison per se, but the Internal Revenue Service putting people in jail for failure to pay their taxes. I can't even begin to understand how some things just never change—they just make some sort of permutation—yet retain the obnoxious aspects of something supposedly discarded.*

"Plain and simple, James exclaimed, this needs to be changed everywhere, immediately, if not sooner!"

So while the pigs became fatter and lazier by the day, the ruling elite Pigs, their Piggiest Party, and their leader Ledig, decided some Pigs were more than equal to others. You can well imagine the anguish of the disfavored Pigs who all of a sudden were relegated to a subservient position... categorized with the animals in common, and lowered to the same social position. Simply accomplished through legislative action, the ruling Pigs, the Piggiest Party, the LARD Legislature and President Ledig, reasoned they should get more of the bounty than the other Pigs, simply because they were in power and controlled the reins of government!

Assuming authority and control became an increasingly easier undertaking; with each succeeding act, the Elitist

Piggiest Party, LARD, and Ledig enacted they became fatter, greedier and meaner with each passing day! As James observed, the empowered forces became increasingly disconnected from the Proletariat they pledged to improve and elevate.

From James' experience, he remembered there are myriad comparisons to this not so subtle, consuming and obtrusive control over the many, by the few. James remembered history as rife with similar happenings within various Communist countries and, surprisingly to many, even in the U.S.A. American legislators were constantly being bribed, *de facto*, by Elite's lobbyists with money, stock options and favors from lobbyists for corporation. Add to this corruption, a "Cadillac" health plan from the government and opulent retirement benefits, which were far too common. James knew too well that in a concept where everything should belong to the Proletariat, the professed ideal always gets skewed when a Communist government is created. What ultimately transpires is political party officials taking special privileges and possessions not enjoyed by the rest of the population! Historically, never has a Communist or socialist government been significantly different; each one has become a complete contradiction and repudiation of the Proletariat myth of everyone being equal! "Apparently Karl Marx and his 'Das Capital' are inherently flawed," James yelled out loud, to no one in particular, while feeling a need to fully express himself.

Since it was illegal to graze or kill your own food, as per the edict of the Piggiest LARD Legislature, the animals had to work to get money to buy their food and pay their rent. Before this the animals lived stress free lives in a paradise. Now the Pig Elites of the LARD Legislature arbitrarily decided the animals, other than the officers in the companies, which basically consisted of the Pigs, should now work for a minimum wage; in essence, their future would become a slave-like type of impoverishment. Meanwhile, the salaries for the Pigs grew... completely disproportionate to the work they provided, and the minimum wages paid to the animals was grossly inadequate to the effort they provided companies, or what was needed for even a bare bones survival.

In light of his recognition, James could not contain his sarcasm as he thought, *This is just too similar to what is happening on my third-dimension Human Earth. I am sure the morphic resonance—projected thoughts carried by energy waves in the atomic field/atoms from my Earth—is "bleeding through to this Earth dimension and detrimentally affecting it, irrespective of the Communist hell that has been concocted within.*

The income disparity caused great friction and animosity by the animals toward the pigs, but anyone who complained was fired and/or jailed or pejoratively referred to as conspiracy theorists... or labeled as malcontented slackers, devoid of motivation and a good work ethic. James remembered a situation similar to this, on his third-dimension Earth, without the jailing scenario, when the CEO of Dunkin Donuts, who made almost $4900 hour, said he could not afford to pay his employees more than the minimum wage! Again, James, unable to dismiss the irony of this situation, conjectured that most likely the Pigs learned this from their human oligarchy counterparts. Irritated by just thinking of flippant remarks by the Dunkin Donuts CEO, James blurted aloud, "Maybe a reversal of roles... to his job being a minimum wage employee in his company... would change his perspective! If not, he should still remain as a minimum wage employee!"

James also reflected back to the "Occupy L.A." in his third-dimension Human Earth and other similar movements where government officials and the mainstream medias constantly marginalized anyone protesting for more equitable wages. Then he considered other campaigns by hotel workers to procure a union contract so they could have better working conditions and higher wages, and how the hotel owners shut down the hotels and laid off the workers, so as to not have to negotiate with them in good faith. James surmised, as he thought his beloved Ann might be listening, *All of this, and more, clearly reveals a disturbing trend of greed where I live and seems to have affected this subdivided animal dimension Earth, Pig Land.*

With the establishment and necessity of jobs came income taxes and the enactment of sales taxes, each considered necessary to support the opulent life styles of the Piggiest Party LARD Legislators and its President, Ledig, The legal subversions served to pile another layer of misery on the animals since they did not even have enough food to eat, and found themselves in a quandary where they were damned if they did pay their taxes, knowing they would not have enough money to buy food on the black market to sustain themselves, and damned if they didn't, whereby they would be imprisoned when it was discovered they were tax scofflaws. Neither scenario was palatable in any way, shape or form. Viewing this James thought, *the taxman cometh and he does not give a shi-ite whether you can pay or not. A pound of flesh must be extracted, if not more.*

This was further compounded with regulatory agencies like the Worker Safety Agency (WSA), akin to OSHA in the human realm of Earth, which became incessant in issuing more regulations that squelched workers' production and the corporate ability to efficiently run their companies, even though the premise of the WSA was worker safety! Yet such so-called safety regulations were ill conceived and in most cases unnecessary. However, these regulations made it even harder for the animal workers to meet the production goals expected of them and made their lives even more stressful.

Since living under a Communist/socialist government is a continually expanding process of accumulating more control, it was not long before the Piggiest Party Legislature, LARD, determined there was a need for a large military presence, including an Army, Navy, Marines and Air Force, supposedly to protect the populace from any aggressive presence, even though there was no imminent threat from anyone in their subdivided dimension.

Obviously, it takes vast amounts of money to support a strong military presence, which inevitably leads to increased taxes and huge amounts of money being wasted on something not really necessary... or was it? Were the Pigs considering an invasion or some other entity to use black operations, where military forces might be engaged in clandestine operations against their own citizens, or provoke war against another country?

James wryly smiled as he muttered, "I certainly could not think of any black operations in the United States other than, well, let's see: there was the Columbine Colorado High School shootings, the Sandy Hook school shootings, the Boston Marathon Massacre, the San Bernardino Massacre, and even in France... the Paris Massacre."

James' smile turned south as he muttered, "Well, I guess I've found many black ops I wish I hadn't. Yet when you keep getting the same descriptions of tall soldiers in black uniforms with military gear and military weapons, spraying bullets around in a methodical fashion, it kind of obliterates the belief domestic and/or Muslim terrorists cause all events. These are cover-ups of major proportions in which the mainstream media has been complicit in ignoring."

Anyway, with more jobs being created, out of a necessity for animals to have food and a place to live, the Pigs and Ledig embarked upon a large industrial revolution, similar to what happened in Europe and the USA in the 1800's and in China, in more recent times... in the subdivided human third-dimension Earth. These industrial revolutions were/are a process of countries switching from an agrarian/agriculture economy to a manufacturing one based on the large-scale production of goods/products. It was a process of rapid industrialization with a concomitant pollution of planet Earth. There was also a rampant abuse of workers putting in sixteen hour-a-day work shifts, dangerous working conditions and paltry wages.

With the revolution and the need to create more jobs, sustainability took a back seat, as did significant amounts of pollution of water, air and ground, likewise. This was bad for the Pigs and the rest of the animals, but for the trees and plants... considerably worse. So Tree Rights for Enlightened Arboriculture (T.R.E.A.) objected vociferously, since they were being adversely affected by being cut down, removed, poisoned and killed by industrial wastes.

The Pigs just laughed at the complaints of the trees and plants and their organization, T.R.E.A, with President Ledig proclaiming, "We are not going to be swayed by a bunch of lowly trees and plants!"

So the decimation of Earth continued—unabated—since the Pigs, their LARD Legislature, and President Ledig all remained oblivious to the fact they were destroying their own planet! As James observed this he also postured the question, "Is this typical of how humans would and have reacted in the past? Maybe Pig Land is trying to outdo us Earth humans!"

The idiocy of this wanton disregard and debauchery of Nature and Natural Law, discussed in *Beyond the Mists of Time: When Trees Ruled the Earth,* was far beyond what the trees and plants could accept, since they knew the whole biosphere would be diminished and eventually destroyed—

and Earth would be made uninhabitable, not only for them but everyone! Unfortunately, the doltish ruling Pigs could not "see the forest from the trees," so to speak, since they were blinded by avarice and extreme greed, just like their human corporate counterparts on the subdivided third-dimension Human Earth.

Making money, hoarding resources and controlling everybody and everything became the Elitist Pig's sole focus! Eventually, the water supplies for the animals became so polluted that many potable water sources became unusable and the animals had to buy bottled water, which became increasingly expensive since the Elitist Pigs and President Ledig had control of all water sources, similar to what the Nestle Corporation had accomplished over the subdivided human realm on Earth! So something that had previously been free and available in Pig Land became expensive and rationed. The crushing economic impact was inescapable, but how this could be a Communist utopia James could fully understand, since utopia denotes only something imaginary. The bigger question of how it could be a Communist paradise completely escaped him because Pig Land was devoid of any vestiges of Paradise, Communist or otherwise!

The air was equally polluted with radiation and heavy metals and greenhouse gases from the burning of coal to generate electrical power. With even more long-term effects, nuclear power plants leaked radiation and experienced operational failures from animal errors and core meltdowns! Unfortunately, those with the least sight, both literally and figuratively, were the very ones given responsibility to run the show and ultimately, run things into the ground... actually a very bare and polluted ground, to wit!

When the animals complained about the state of affairs stemming from the long term effects of the power plants and how free water was no longer available to them, the Pig CEO of Eltsen Corp, Peter Beckbra, who had participated in the corruption of all potable water sources controlled by the LARD legislature and President Ledig, proclaimed, "Water should not be free. Everyone should have to pay for it!" Of course, for the animals that had never paid to drink water before, this was just more evidence at how far things had degenerated from the essential perfection, wherein they previously lived and where everything was free! The feeling prevailed that the initial promises of the Elitist Pigs and President Ledig to create "Heaven on Earth" were in fact without merit or substance; replaced by a world where everything had to be purchased and included a close scrutiny and governance of the animals.

The previous paradise they lived in was gone, just as were God-given freedoms and liberties, including the God-given sovereignty over all animals and governmental authority and the right of unlimited and unrestricted expression, including speech and written communications. Ever so slowly and subtly, as with all totalitarian Communist or socialist governments, the Elitist Pigs, led by President Ledig proclaimed sovereignty over all animals and supplanted God as the ultimate authority and rule. This was a mere formality, since *de facto*, it was already the case!

Alas! Not only had the Elitist Pigs changed the whole sovereignty equation, they refused to even acknowledge and respect their Creator as the superior presence on Planet Earth! As James encountered this he uttered out loud, trying to summon the presence of Ann, "Such is the arrogance of Communists and Socialists. Their ignorance in these matters is legendary! Even more than the smugness is the failure to acknowledge the supremacy of our Creator but this is de rigueur with Communists. They foolishly believe they can assume the godhead, yet so far nary a Communist government has even approximated such! I am still waiting for this to occur but I would put heavy money against it."

Sadly, throughout history, in the human realm under totalitarian Communism with a Socialist agenda, James never found the system to function better than that which the animals of Pig Land experienced. Unfortunately for the citizens of Pig Land, catastrophes became common, manufactured or created both internally and externally, just to keep the animals from rebelling against the Pig Land government. Either it was domestic terrorists in the subdivided animal realm that needed to be suppressed—or the human kind—who supposedly threatened the animal way of life.

As James could clearly see, each crises was created by black operations mercenaries who were funded by off-the-books-revenue paid to mercenary groups, similar to The Craft Group, a.k.a. Blackwater Group, in the subdivided human Earth... or to churn things up by paid radical animal elements, akin to Taliban, Al Queda, or ISIS and ISIL in existence on the subdivided human Earth. The names of these radical elements was less important than the fact they were being funded by President Ledig's government to keep things chaotic and the animals off balance and easily manipulated. Glaringly, the parallels to James' Earth were impossible for him to ignore.

Another obvious element to the chain of events was a misdirected ploy to ensure the animals would not realize how bad their lives had become, and less likely to protest against events transpiring around and to them! The ruling Pigs and President Ledig understood the dynamic: animals who were in fear would not think rationally and would never question the veracity of the statements being made, and would be more inclined to eagerly beg to be protected by the government! Unwittingly then, the animals played beautifully into the hands of the government and became their own worst enemies in the process!

Always, without exception, due to the natural and growing unhappiness of the citizens existing under President Ledig's Communist government, the anticipated results included low worker production, increased stress and high state expenses for a health care system, which could not be maintained and sustained in a manner beneficial to the animals.

The inevitable had occurred... the governmental system itself had created the very unhappiness in the lives of its citizens that caused the maladies attached to emotional and physical trauma! Also inevitable was the amount of worker stress and unhappiness led to an unnatural amount of medical problems that over time ultimately overloaded the medical system! No one should have been surprised by the introduction of rationed care, since the entire medical system became over burdened and unable to keep up with the overwhelming number of medical cases and claims generated! Even the disenfranchised pigs sat sadly, shaking their heads in realization of how far things had degenerated from the health and bliss in which the animals had formerly lived.

Our story of the stress, and emotional and physical trauma experienced by the animals provides a natural segue to the subject of the transitions in healthcare. When the animals lived off the land in the unfettered Earth, there was virtually no sickness, since they were immersed in the Divine forces of Nature, as opposed to the stress involved with living in an urban environment! Along with civilization and urbanization came a world of animals chronically ill and experiencing many forms of disease. The diminished health was caused in part by eating refined foods always found in so called civilized cultures. Even more than the degraded quality of the food, however, the stress experienced by the animals, due to working in dead end jobs and filled with stress from unrealistic production goals expected by the Pig CEO's, was the bigger causational factor of the previously related spiraling descent into sickness.

One of the benefits, if you could really call it such, was each citizen's right to Socialized Medical Services (SMS). The benefit was really a double-edged sword however, since previously, no animal required medical services. Where they experienced only happiness and had no stress, the sickness and disease they experienced stemming from raw, negative emotions simply did not exist. Additionally, such medical services were not really top quality medical care, and patients experienced long waits to get a doctor visit or referred to a hospital. While the LARD Legislator's and President Ledig were provided top quality quality medical care, the animals had nothing that remotely resembled the type of care normally afforded a king or a queen. If any animal complained about the disparity, they were not denied care per se, but they just rarely, if ever, received any medical services, as they had quietly been blackballed!

Thinking back on the ramifications of having been black-balled, it might not have been such a deprivation as one might consider; the treatments used by the medical establishment had many side effects. Patients experienced iatrogenesis, which is from a Greek word that refers to the effects resulting from healthcare professionals or products or services promoted as beneficial to health, but not really being so. It also was related to the side effects from medicines taken from their natural state and extracting only the active ingredients there from, leading to adverse reactions from the medicines prescribed to heal. It got to the point where multiple medicines had to be prescribed just to deal with the successive side effects, causing reaction from one medicine that led to being given another, and then the next, ad infinitum!

Although quite evident, few realized the negative side effects were the result of taking natural foods and herbs the animals had always used, and the drug becoming toxic when pharmaceutical companies synthesized the active ingredient from the complex of the food or herb to make it patentable—the very buffering compounds installed by the Creator—had been removed in the process.

James knew greedy people, blinded by avarice, never let something like dangerous side effects stop them producing things that are overpriced and yet chemically unbalanced and capable only of dealing with the symptoms—not curing anything! Some of the medicines, including anti-depressants, had serious side effects; for example, if the animals stopped taking the medicines they could actually become very violent. How that could be a benefit for anyone, was hard for James to fathom! All of these so-called health practices were the result of so-called medicines, which treated nothing more than the symptoms of sickness and disease, but never the real physical cause, or more importantly, emotional components attached thereto. James, being a doctor of natural medicine, found all of this easy to understand!

Perhaps the most egregious example of this was when patients were diagnosed with cancer, they were subject to oncology protocols that were not only expensive, but debilitated the animal's body with extremely expensive heavy metals from chemotherapy, radiation burns to their internal organs, and the removal of tumors. The end result was not a cure; these unnatural invasions into a body spread the cancer even more. The doctors seemed oblivious to the fact tumors had, by the Creator's design, a designated purpose to localize the cancer virus/fungus in the body, the removal of which only served to spread the cancer more. Very few doctors, if any, considered detoxifying the animals' bodies to remove the cancer's causative factors, and even fewer considered the emotional factors linked to the disease. This issue was rather mystifying to James; there were studies into epigenetics—that addressed the changes in organisms caused by modifying gene expression rather than altering the genetic code itself—that proved this link! For sure, certain and most true, none of the oncology protocols ever cured cancer, they just suppressed it for a certain period of time, only to have it return with a vengeance!

Food, housing, employment, and medicine... the repressive, totalitarian Communist government instituted by the Elite Piggiest Legislature, LARD, and President Ledig, knew no bounds to its intrusiveness into the affairs of animal families. The next step was to intervene in cases of domestic marital violence, when in fact there was little or none, which ultimately included the taking of children from animal families based on the most minimal amounts of evidence. If there was any disciplining of animal family children by the animal parents, even when justified, the children were summarily whisked away from the parents and put in the custody of state social services. The state generated vast amounts of revenue with this tactic by charging the parents for the care provided to their children, even though for the most part the children would have been better and more lovingly cared for by their parents. The newest motto of the state was: *We know how to better take care of you and your children than you parents do!*

Thus, it was no surprise to the animals or James that soon thereafter the government outlawed the home schooling of children, even on religious grounds, since it greatly feared animals that were able to think independently of government standards foisted upon them. Yet, in a parallel Earth-dimension, a similar replication of another Earth, discussed in the String Theory and the Membrane Theory from Quantum Physics and Quantum Mechanics, other animals lived in very different circumstances, even though facing many of the same challenges as the animals in Pig Land.

This multi-dimensional Earth was something James had studied and understood there were at least fourteen dimensions stacked in virtually the same space; within these dimensions are parallel places that mimic each other, not always in complete detail but at the least with many similarities. James, however, was much more concerned about the fate of the Pig Land animals as he felt he might have a vested interest in their future fate. Soon he would have an epiphany that would reveal just how true that was.

CHAPTER TWO

A Parallel Earth With a Lot Less Poo You Would Find in a Zoo

——— ·⸙⋆⸙· ———

MEANWHILE, IN A parallel Earth-dimension, connected to Pig Land with a trans-dimensional energy connection, kind of like strings of electromagnetic energy, was a place known as Natural Land. James viewed therein animals that lived in the state of bliss to which they had always been accustomed. In this parallel Earth-dimension there was also an attempt by the Elitist Pigs to install themselves as the overlords of the Animal Kingdom, however, things worked out very differently in this scenario.

The other animals were extremely suspicious of any specific animal group who made the claim they could make something already perfect, as per Aleph Kaf Aleph, the 7th Name of God from Exodus of *The Torah*, better than the paradise the Creator had already provided for them! Even here, the Pig Elites talked about creating a Communist Utopia. Fortunately, the other animals were perceptive enough to know utopia actually referred to a perfect dream, but they were also cognizant of currently living in a perfect paradise that was close at hand; existing already. This proffered airy-fairy dream had little attraction for them.

Enough of the animals had been exposed to the idea of an inherently perfect creation so as not to be bamboozled into falling for the outrageous claims of the Elitist Pigs! In light of this fact, the Pigs were marginalized and relegated to being perceived as inferior by all the other animal groups, because their promoted concept of a Communist Utopia was perverted and deeply flawed. Further, the Pigs were warned, in no uncertain terms, they and their offspring would be executed if they ever attempted to establish their nefarious idea of controlling and enslaving the other animals

James considered it was the higher dimension this Earth occupied by the animals of Natural Land that accounted for a higher level of consciousness and perception because the animals lived in a fourth and fifth-dimensional construct. Virtually every animal meditated for at least half an hour each day; it infused them from the mediation sessions with altered and elevated brainwaves in the alpha and theta range. It was these alpha and theta brainwaves, especially at the theta level, which accounted for enhanced psychic abilities leading to the animals exhibiting more intuition, telepathy, clairvoyance, etc. This practice and its results meant this collective of animals could not be bamboozled and misdirected.

The animals residing in Natural Land, on the alternate Earth, followed the templates of Nature and Natural Law, as per the book *Beyond the Mists of Time: When Trees Ruled the Earth*... and in Henry David Thoreau's *On Walden Pond*. As they existed in Human Earth of the third-dimension, even though none of them had been exposed to either of these books, the animals inherently understood the natural laws, with a clarity unperceived by today's humans. They also operated in a higher dimension of being and consciousness than those existing on the Pig Land controlled Earth, pursuant to the brainwaves elicited from their assiduous meditation, which had positive effects extending into the rest of their lives.

Eventually, in a subdivided-dimension occupied by Pig Land, Hyena Land would be formed, where inhabitants followed Totalitarian Communist and socialist ways. Therein, animals were routinely exploited as were Earth's resources, and everything in Hyena Land languished in the mediocrity of the third-dimension and the inherent limitations therein! Many of the limitations had to do with the denser energies in the third-dimension, the result of atoms moving at a slower rate, and which made everything harder to achieve and did not lend well to higher consciousness, perceptions and prescience.

On the third-dimension of Earth's Pig Land existed the greedy Elitist Pigs, including families commonly recognized as the Rothschild's, Rockefeller's, Mellon's, Morgan's, Ford's, and Bush's... all of whom were known to have worked in conjunction with the LARD Legislature and President Ledig and various monarchs in Europe, to control and enslave as many people as possible. These families were allowed to amass immense wealth because they were socialists who wanted all animals subjugated to their authority and to be used and abused as labor slaves, just like President Ledig and the LARD Legislature. It should be noted there also existed a human counterpart for each of these animal families in the subdivided third-dimension Earth, which James considered genetic aberrations, because of their unmitigated greed and lust for power, and a complete rejection of Natural Law, as well as inbreeding among the elitist families.

James found it ironic and inherently unjust that less than one percent of the population controlled 90% of the wealth and resources on Earth, either directly or indirectly—through interlocking directorates—individual companies that are linked together—vertically and/or horizontally—creating monopolies. The ability to establish internal strongholds was made possible by becoming part of the Elitist Pig inner circle. The Pigs, who had learned this aberrant and repugnant behavior from their human counterparts in the subdivided third-dimension Earth, from morphic resonance rather than actual physical contact with the humans, became more than adept at subjugating and abusing the common people... the masses... the Proletariat!

Irrespective of the continuing turmoil experienced in Pig Land, James sensed the animals in Natural Land, a thriving parallel Earth, lived in a modern day Garden of Eden, or if you will, a Paradise Found in contradistinction to John Milton's book, *Paradise Lost*! Living in something better than a libertarian republic, actually more like a benign Anarchy, a Divine Manifestation, if you will, where everyone had the opportunity to live without the intervention of governmental authority and everyone inherently understood the natural order of things. Those living in this thriving land experienced none of the inverted issues of sovereignty that manifested in Pig Land, within the totalitarian Communist Pig Land Earth, which claimed absolute power over everyone and everything; essentially "playing" God!

Everyone was essentially happy and the emotional and epigenetic factors that caused the rampant sickness and disease found in Pig Land, simply could not and did not exist; nor did poverty or hunger. There was no domestic violence, since every animal was at peace; everyone was amply bathed in the calming energies of Nature. The accumulation of positive traits and behaviors made their lives run smoothly. Additionally, there was no intervention by the state in the lives of children and their parents because there was no need for one! Religions filled with contradictory beliefs were also deemed unnecessary in a place ruled by Nature and Natural Law.

Inhabitants experienced no police brutality because there were no police! With no military presence, there were no wars. Furthermore, there was no killing, other than for food,

26

because there were no guns—or a need to possess them. James considered this being the only effective form of gun control—the absence of all weapons in a society, including those normally possessed by a government, through its police and military forces! Unfortunately, the human counterparts of the animals, who favored gun control, were not prescient enough to realize if some people had guns, there would always be gun violence and criminals would always have guns, as certitude! James knew there was no known exception to this!

Natural Land, of course, embodied the concepts of: *Zeitgeist,* functionally known as a living sustainably where the sharing of all resources was of prominent importance, first considered in the 1960's and attaining a resurgence in the twenty first century. These ideas, as James well knew, are portrayed in the *Thrive* documentary, which sets out a plan of a sustainable, green Earth where there is no hoarding of resources and a general sharing thereof, just as exists in Nature; and the movie *Avatar,* which not only embodies disarmament by all of the World's nations but also a sharing of all resources, equally, be that money or natural resources or food; and the book, *Beyond the Mists of Time: When Trees Ruled the Earth,* which discusses how things operate in the realm of Nature and how to use this knowledge and the wisdom of very ancient civilizations to create an equitable and sustainable Earth, with an equity and equality among all people.

James viewed this as a perfect combination of concepts and in reality, a non-totalitarian, non-communist, and non-socialist alternative to sharing, where the higher consciousness and knowledge of individuals are supreme to dysfunctional governmental structures that never deliver what they promise, anyway, at any time in the history of Planet Earth or anywhere else. James pondered for a moment his one known exception to this, namely Libya, where the leader, Mommar Kaddafi, provided for his people like no other leader in the history of the third dimension Earth. James had watched as Kaddafi was assassinated in a covert black operation on his Earth and the Elitist Pigs did the same thing in their subdivided animal Earth dimension, as they did not want any existing examples of a thriving government actually caring for its people, to be known by the animals! Before all of this turmoil there was an incessant propaganda campaign to demonize Kaddafi, so President Ledig could rationalize and justify his killing of the great leader. Ledig's actions buried the great deeds Kaddafi bestowed upon his populace, including universal health care, free college education, no interest loans to purchase houses and many infrastructure improvements to Libya, including a vast network of water canals to bring the desert to bloom. So the Elite Pigs lived by the motto: *If you cannot compete with something, it is better to eliminate and exterminate it.* That they did, and more... sending mercenaries into Libya to completely dismantle and destabilize the previous Kaddafi government.

Meanwhile, in the totalitarian Pig Land Communist Earth, the Pig Legislature, LARD, had instituted a strict gun control under the guise of protecting the animal population from the ravages of gun violence. Many of the animals supported the policy until they realized the criminals still had guns and the crime rate was even higher than before gun control — primarily because the citizenry was unarmed and unable to defend themselves. Once again, the Communist Pigs could not deliver what they promised; just delivering more of the same hollow assurances, which seemed not to faze President Ledig! This was because the so-called promises were a deliberate guise to open the door for more control over the animal populace and increased subservience to the Pig Land government.

Eventually, upon hearing of the plight of their brother animals in the repressive Pig Land Earth, the Natural Land animals would make a trip through a time portal or worm hole, known to most as an Einstein-Rosen Bridge—a topological shortcut connecting two separate points in space time—to liberate their compatriots. They could not bear to know their brothers and sisters on the parallel earth were bound in the slavery of totalitarian Communism and the drudgery and misery associated with governmental practices thrust upon the Proletariat of Pig Land! However, the time had to be propitious for this mission to succeed and at this point in time, James could see it was not... and knew the animal leaders of Natural Land knew this also!

CHAPTER THREE

Back to the Pee and a Lot of Pooh, Too!

—————

PEOPLE LIKE GENERAL George Washington are few and far between and really as likely to appear as a Blue Moon that happens once every three years. Interestingly enough, General Washington really did not even want to be the first president of the United States of America, and very reluctantly agreed to accept the job because of the wide spread belief he was the best person possible to fill the position. The great Thomas Jefferson, who actually undertook a smear campaign to defeat John Adams in his race for the presidency and the ascendance thereto, could not even claim the significance of not wanting the power of the presidency. His actions here would betray any words to the contrary, aside from him being an important president in the genesis of the United States!

James tied his thoughts to the Elitist Pigs in power on the Communist Pig Land Earth, including the nefarious President Ledig, whose egos expanded at a rate commensurate to their rapidly expanding girth and the wealth they accumulated, which, by the way, completely violated the basic principles of Communism, as expounded in *The Communist Manifesto*! Certainly, President Ledig never even remotely exhibited the properties of George Washington, even though he too professed to not having a desire for power. James deliberated in his mind, *I sure wish the animals of Pig Land could see this exact situation happening in the realm of the Pig's human counterparts in a subdivided Earth third-dimension Human Land, where I live. They have the disadvantage of not being able to observe the control mechanisms used by the Cabal, known as the Illuminati; they are complicit in all of this dysfunction known as Communism, and are not illumined, as the Illuminati name denotes in Latin. Can not the animals see the Elitist Pigs and President Ledig were never kind or generous to anyone other than their own compatriots, often in the least amount and even at times resorted to killing their own kind?*

This deliberation helped James realize the animals were consciously unaware of this since they were dimensionally separated; yet they were still being affected by the aberrant behavior of the Human Elites, through the effect of morphic resonance and the power and persuasion of the thoughts transmitted into this morphic memory field. Eventually, the animals would be more aware of how the thoughts and actions, morphic fields of energy, from other dimensions, could and did, impact them.

Anyway, when the time came for the election of a new president, everyone thought it was a foregone conclusion—the wife of the sitting Pig President, President Ledig, would be elected, even though the president had a sexual affair with one of his interns! The president claimed he only had oral sex and so he ...*did not really have sex with that woman!* This debacle caused a great scandal that almost got the president impeached but the LARD Legislature refused to do so since they were themselves "in bed" with President Ledig. The cuckold wife, nicknamed Hillbilly, had garnered great sympathy and respect because she stood by her man. Hillbilly had the attitude she was entitled to be President and was very deserving of such. Make no mistake, although she carried the moniker of

Hillbilly, she was an astute politician who was very cunning and would never hesitate to assassinate any rival who stood in the path to her objective.

Yet, in an unexpected turn of events, it was interesting how a freshman black Pig Land legislator, Karab, started to pick up momentum and turned the tide against the president's wife, because he was even more astute, cunning and ruthless than Hillbilly. It was widely believed Karab would have more empathy for the animal populace and make things better for them, since he was of African descent and a minority in his own country of Pig Land. In a landslide, not only did Karab win his party's nomination but the presidential election, to wit! That might have been propitious for Karab, but it only ensured a continued misery for the animal populace, as they would soon discover.

As James viewed this travesty, he saw the inescapably direct similarities between the Pig Land election and one on the subdivided third-dimension Human Earth, involving Hillary Clinton and Barak Obama and even the background character, former president Bill Clinton. James laughed out loud and proclaimed, "There seems to be enough dysfunctional politicians for any and all dimensions. The stench of all of this is most disagreeable but that is what occurs in the political arena—a lot of bullshit, which is only useful for plowing into the ground and making a soil more fertile. As for having any value for the people, well..."

After the election followed the traditional State of the Union message, where President Karab recited his plans to help the plight of the animals. He kept very few of his promises, other than to make healthcare accessible for everyone. Unfortunately, in the process of meeting his promises, he made medical care even more expensive for everyone. With no end to the surprises delivered by President Karab, shortly after the election it was discovered he was not even a natural born citizen and not even remotely qualified to be president. Oh, the president did indeed provide a birth certificate to authenticate his citizenship, but the serial number did not coincide within the numerical sequence of numbers used when he was born!

Upon taking in all of this, James thought, *This is exactly what Donald Trump had brought to our attention with Barak Obama and yet he was labeled as a 'kook!' Unfortunately there is little new under the Sun since the American people have had to endure a Circus of the Bizarre, and all the while have been pilloried whenever they questioned the veracity of or even the ability of our recent president to ever tell the truth. Yet the Republicons and Dumbacrats are all complicit in this mediocrity as they allow it to exist and remain the norm!"*

In relation to a growing list of broken promises and less-than-truthful statements made and positions taken by President Karab, an interesting and disingenuous propaganda campaign was undertaken to defend him, and those who questioned the president's qualifications were labeled "conspiracy theorists!" Most of the animals resonated with this conspiracy idea, even though the facts bespoke otherwise! The Elitist Pigs controlled media outlets, circled their wagons around the president and constantly excoriated anyone who would be gullible enough to believe in a conspiracy theory, which was in fact, actually a "conspiracy reality!"

Considering this, James conjectured, "I have always held some doubt as to the complete validity and operation of morphic fields and morphic resonance but with what I am seeing now, how can I question there are "bleed throughs" where information and experiences are being shared back and forth between the various dimensions, parallel and higher?"

"Further, this tends to prove the concept from Quantum Mechanics that where are all things are interconnected and there is a non duality operating in the Cosmos, meaning I am you and you are me, and we are all together, cuckucahu!"

There were more things related to the president that could not stand muster or really hold any water: never was there found even a trace of credibility when the president listed several colleges he attended and yet no one who attended those same colleges when the president purported to have done so who could attest to him actually being there. The breach of credibility grew even wider when the president was discovered to have more than one permutation of his name. Everything surrounding this president seemed extremely fishy, yet he seemed to have a Teflon coating that worked as an armor, which did not allow anything to stick to him, including illegal black operations (covert operations off the government books), and other events similar to ISIS, Libya, Syria, Iraq, Afghanistan and the 9-11 Twin Towers demolition; all these operations had mirrored counterparts on the third-dimension Human Earth!

As was mentioned earlier, the Elitist Pigs of Pig Land had a constant series of manufactured crises, be they domestic or external, to keep the animals distracted by just how bad their lives were and how much things had degenerated for the Proletariat! James kept thinking the animals would eventually see through this; actually, they did appear to sense something was very wrong, but they had not quite reached the point of overt resistance! Hence, because of the animal's inability to perceive the synchronicities that were common in all of these events, they were inadvertently responsible for sealing their own fate! As James opined, "They are culpable of poor judgment or lack thereof; each day seems to bring another fairy tale to believe... unicorn explanations of things that suspend rational belief!"

Other events occurred in the realm of the animals in another dimensional subdivision on the third-dimension Earth;

namely, amongst the wild animals, the Lions fought the Hyenas, to keep them from usurping power over all the other wild animals. The Hyenas were most cowardly when fighting alone, but were very ferocious when fighting in a pack. Case in point: their only mode of fighting was in packs—the mode of cowards. An individual Lion was easily more ferocious and powerful than an individual Hyena, but could not match power and force over groups of Hyenas. Eventually, the Hyenas "carried the day" since the Lions seemed incapable of massing their forces and fighting as a unit! Each lion seemed to want to be the King, in keeping with their King of the Jungle moniker and having only kings and no soldiers... no credible resistance to the Hyenas could be mustered.

The Pigs ultimately sent emissaries through a time portal, or vortex, to help the Hyenas with setting up their government, which was the totalitarian Communist model, as in Pig Land. So right away, due to the inherent flaws and limitations associated with the concept of Communism, James knew there would be no ultimate benefit for the Proletariat of wild animals, and realized things would quickly degenerate into numerous miasmas, with nothing but misery for the wild animals, while the Hyenas lived a life of luxury and privilege—following in the footsteps of their counterparts, the slovenly Pig Elites!

Meanwhile, on the parallel Earth of Natural Land, the animals continued to enjoy their Heaven on Earth. Unlike what happened in the third-dimension Earth of Pig Land and Hyena Land, the Natural Land animals thwarted the Hyenas attempt to subjugate the other animals. The Lions united forces and boldly informed the Hyenas that they, as well as their offspring would be eaten, if they ever considered such a nefarious plan. As James considered what was transpiring, it became clear to him this bold force may well have occurred because a morphic field of thought resonance had been first established by the domesticated animals to thwart the diabolical plans proposed by the Pigs in Natural Land! In retrospect, many things became clear to him, and what the action on the part of the Lions really revealed was the power of thought and its ability and means to shape and fashion what happens in parallel civilizations. This knowledge would be useful in the future to help oust the Communist Pigs and Hyenas from power, both in Pig Land and Hyena Land!

From James' rather detached perspective, the existence of morphic fields and the morphic resonance there from, in the power of a distinct energy field having an effect on things and events, showed him the relationship to a previous comment about the Natural Land Animals having to wait for the right time to help their oppressed brethren. Unfortunately, in the meantime, the domestic and wild animals would find even more misery along the way for them in a third dimension Earth! James exclaimed, to no one in particular, or so he thought, "There's too much similarity to what the Pig Land and Hyena Land animals are experiencing and what is happening on the Earth in which I live!" Little did James know, someone was listening... someone about whom he cared very much. Actually, he was feeling her presence! Who might that be?

CHAPTER FOUR

A Whole Lot More...
Even Some Gore!

————————

AS NOTED EARLIER, one of the problems associated in the Pig Land and Hyena Land controlled subdivided third-dimension Earth, was the existence and operation as a third-dimension planet. The Natural Land Earth, which maintained a Heaven on Earth system, was in fact a fourth-dimension reality, and transiting into a fifth-dimension reality. The higher the dimension, it seemed the more Divine things were... or at least close thereto!

Why would the dimension of an Earth make any difference, you ask? James was ready to answer that exact question as he stated, "To be scientifically correct, there are nine geometric forms of creation on the atomic level, as per Valery P. Kondrtov's *Geometry of a Uniform Field*, discussed in Chapter one of *A Map to Healing and Your Essential Divinity Through Theta Consciousness*. These geometric forms occur in all dimensions but become more complexly assembled and distributed in each successively higher dimension, with a denser, more widely arrayed manifestation of the nine geometric forms on the atomic level of creation, With each ascending dimension, things become less material and more apparent in their true energy form(s); and in these higher energy fields, humans demonstrate more psychic abilities and their brainwaves enter a calmer and more creative level, in the alpha and theta range. It is these psychic abilities, manifested in the elevated dimensions that acted like a filter and a gate and which did not allow the Natural Land and Wild Land animals to be bamboozled by the nefarious plans of the elitist, oligarchic animals on the parallel Earth of Natural Land."

James continued his thoughts, as he was sure Ann was listening, *So with this setting of the stage, so to speak, the power of having highly developed psychic abilities, that comes from the more evolved brainwaves of alpha and theta, lies in the inability of people to deceive each other, as their developed psychic abilities alert them when someone is lying and/or being disingenuous! The importance of this fact is that not only are people more creative, they are also better problem solvers, as well!*

"Most likely, then," James continued in a bemused state, "the inability to perceive blatant or subtle lies, and deeply disingenuous presentments of promises, accounted for Communist governments being instituted in the third-dimension Earth and why the nefarious schemes were not manifested in the fourth and fifth-dimension Earth... because of more developed psychic abilities!"

In fact, there were a number of people who were certain the third-dimension Earth Pig Land and Hyena Land, was ready to transition to a fourth-dimension operating system, likewise, but at this point in time, with the unrest and demoralized communities, it certainly did not seem evident, apparent, or even possible. The act of moving into higher dimensional operating systems was possible through several factors, including more hyper dimensional, torsional, electromagnetic energy being directed to Earth from the center of the Milky Way Galaxy, actually measurable with an electrometer, with corresponding verification of this from Richard Hoagland, of the Enterprise Mission, and French and Russian scientists!

Also, with the Sun combusting at a higher temperature, due to a hydrogen cloud from an exploded star—where the Sun was currently positioned—more heat being emitted meant more energy entering Earth! So the effect of this—heat—energy was little by little pushing the lower dimension Earth into a higher dimensional position. James knew it was exactly the same occurrences that are the catalyst, which makes atoms move faster and exhibit higher dimensional characteristics, as per Valery P. Kondratov's *Geometry of a Uniform Field*! Simply put, faster moving and orbiting atoms equates to the manifestation of the higher dimensions. Of all of these foregoing things, James had considerable knowledge.

Meanwhile, on the Pig Land and Hyena Land Communist based socialist Earth, everyone started to realize the Earth was getting hotter. The fact was undeniable, but rather than attributing it to natural causes—of the Sun getting hotter and distributing that heat to Earth in kind—an ex-Vice President, Ozone Al Bore, in Pig Land Earth, dreamed up the idea the changes were attributable to greenhouse gases, written about in his book, *An Inconvenient Truth*. Upon viewing this James could not refrain from quipping aloud, hoping to entertain and entice Ann, "Oh yeah, Ozone Al, mentor of the stupids! It is so far beyond being incomprehensible how anyone could find any veracity in the words of a career politician, who has never been a scientist and never run a business. I guess his credentials come from Uranus and I am not talking about the planet!"

The real inconvenient truth was the Sun was never even remotely considered as causation for the warming. Some of the animals from Pig Land and Hyena Land started to see through the greenhouse gas—global warming— scenario once it was proposed that a carbon tax was to be paid to the Nations United, a United Nations equivalent in the Pig Land subdivided Earth, to what had been imposed on the humans on Earth, a large bureaucratic Communist front organization. Funds from the tax were to be used to mitigate the supposed global warming phenomenon. In the end, the entire concept was nothing more than a ploy to more deeply impoverish the already abused and oppressed animal population!

Interestingly enough, the tax was ultimately enacted, but the heat on Earth continued to increase, even though greenhouse gases were substantially reduced! James was laughing his ass off as he considered, *Is this the last laugh on Mr. Bore? Are all the claims of reducing global warming more akin to the stench of flatulence gases?* Ann was stunned into silence by James' sardonic *thoughts*, but she was ultimately driven to laugh at his tirade.

What was hard to laugh at was the Pig Land and Hyena Land governments decided to start spraying chemical aerosols into the atmosphere, containing Aluminum oxide, Barium oxide, Strontium 90 and other toxins, supposedly to lower ambient temperature on Earth. The animal populaces were not consulted about this and when they started to notice streams of chemicals in the skies, laid down by jet airliners, which slowly dispersed themselves... they grew suspicious about what was going on. When the animals queried their legislatures, they were summarily told, 'What you see is only the contrails that naturally emanate from jet engines."

The reality was quite contrary to this lame explanation as people started to realize the jet contrails will completely disperse into invisibility yet the chemical cocktail being sprayed into the skies was not comparable and lasted for hours at a time. Yes in fact, the chemical aerosols did lower the

Earth's ambient temperature, but at a cost of health related illnesses from the toxic chemicals being sprayed into the skies. These illnesses would increase the burden on an already over-laden socialist health care system. Additionally, the chemicals seemed to prevent normal amounts of rainfall from occurring and they also created a synthetic ionosphere that allowed the Pig Land and Hyena Land governments to more effectively dispense brain-washing signals to control the thoughts of the animals, so they would remain complacent.

The stark contrast with this experience and what happened on the parallel Heaven on Earth on Natural Land Earth was that the more evolved animals welcomed the heating on their Earth. They knew although the seas might rise, and the heat from the Sun would push their planet into an even higher dimension, which they intuitively knew was a very good thing. The animals on Natural Land Earth were further aware that when the earth started heating up dramatically, there was a high probability of an impending Ice Age to follow. Going back in time and reviewing a climate model of the last Ice Age ascertained this.

As James considered all of this out loud, he stated, "I wonder when my fellow humans will figure this out? Am I living on the planet of the stupids, myself?" To James' astonishment, he thought he could feel the presence of Ann in his vicinity, something he had sensed earlier.

Just then Ann laughed out loud and spoke to her beloved James, "I know as a certitude you are not stupid James, since I have been watching you put things together about the oppressed and free animals... but your plane—your dimension of Earth—seems to be surrounded by an energy field of stupidity. That is why I died and moved on, the stupidity rampant on your Earth was stifling my creativity, education and spiritual growth."

James was giddy with delight that Ann had graced him with the presence of her angelic form, and heartily laughing he replied, "Ah, ha! I knew you were hanging around watching my anguish trying to figure out how to help these animals mired in the Communist Circus of the Bizarro! Maybe you have seen further ahead than I have and know how things will turn out? I must also add your assessment of Earth is the most acerbic thing I have ever heard you say!"

Ann smirked as she spoke, "Well, I have seen the future, but I am not sharing it all with you, because I do not want to interfere with the space-time continuum, hahahaha! One thing I will tell you, however, the aerosol spraying is being suspended, at least for the time being."

Somewhat exasperated James exclaimed, "GFR, I need a break here!"

Ann quickly retorted, "I only mend bones, I do not break them, ha! Just wait and see what happens!"

Actually, help was on the way for third-dimension Earth and it would be naturally pushed into a fourth and fifth-dimension Earth; this would be a good thing... a very good thing, even though James did not know such yet!

In the meantime, however, more misery was unleashed on the subdivided third-dimension Earth of Pig Land and Hyena Land. The Hyena's decreed no animal could graze or hunt for its food and all food would be centrally distributed through the highly-inefficient Communist government, and just as one might figure, similar to the situations experienced at the hands of the Pig Land Communist government. At first there were sporadic shortages and then chronic shortfalls. The wild animals were given script to buy their food at no charge, yet the script only bought ten days worth of food.

Again, history was repeating itself in what transpired? Out of necessity, a black market for food sprang into existence, to keep the animals and their progeny from starving to death, which was really controlled by the Hyena Land government. The same thing happened in Pig Land and in the country of Cuba and North Korea on the Human Earth, to wit! Additionally, the animals did not even know where their food was coming from, and it was hard to recognize the exact constituents in the food. Some of the foods were genetically modified crops that caused digestion problems and leaky gut syndrome. Other foods were laced with manures, which only pigs would really like or gravitate to. Viewing the food situation, James relayed his thoughts to Ann, *This seems to be a twist on Soylent Green! You remember, the 1973 American Metrocolor science fiction film?*

Ann laughingly responded, *You are considerably more correct than you know as there are dead human bodies and "road kill" contained in the so called food, so it is indeed very much like Soylent Green.*

James needed little time to react to Ann's comments as he was getting a sick feeling in his stomach yet he managed to blurted out, "I guess these animals have worse than a shitty existence, then, as it were!"

Following an inevitable pattern, the Hyena Land animals complained about this state of affairs, but were told just what the Pig Land animals had also been promised, "Don't worry, this is only a temporary glitch and soon, things will be much better!" James just shook his head back and forth as he listened to yet another hollow promise proclaimed by the Elitists in both Pig Land and Hyena Land, as is all the piffle and propaganda Communist, socialistic governments forcibly and subtlety foist upon their subjects! Yet let it be known... the Hyena Elites always had more than enough to eat and they were becoming as fat and slovenly as their counterpart Pigs and they were not eating the Soylent Green equivalent, laced with manures, which the Pigs actually craved!

James was rather amazed as he watched an interesting synchronistic scenario play out; the Pig Land and Hyena Land animals complained about the horrible conditions under which they lived. The reaction by Pig Land and Hyena Land leaders, who feared an armed revolt against their rule, instituted gun control, as was mentioned earlier, under the innocuous guise the people would be safer from criminal elements and acts of crime. In fact, there was some crime in these realms, for sure, but not nearly so much as the government claimed in its solidly controlled media sources!

Many of the animals thought gun control would be a good idea, despite their horrible plight in life, but they were astonished to find violent crime escalated under gun control — guns were of course taken from those who feared not complying; however, as should have been expected, the criminals had retained their weapons! James compared this to what happened in the last Human Earth country to enact gun control, Australia, as he thought, *I remember the crime rate soared right after this occurred. Even when the citizens in Australia complained about the subsequent increase in crimes, the politicians and government just blew them off.*

In truth, the criminals really did not want to lead a life of crime, but rather, felt they had no choice since they were without food and basic necessities of life and since they were not allowed to start their own businesses, they saw little other choices available for them to survive! "How many times and in how many ways does the lesson have to be learned about seeking to create a utopian, Communist country?" James opined to Ann. *The irony of this is too severe to be ignored! Utopian it might be, but not remotely anything resembling Paradise, at least for the animal populace at large.*

Ann laughingly shared, *I am reading your fertile mind, James, and Communism only leads to misery. It is never found in any dimension beyond the third one and has no place in paradise or Heaven, for that matter!*

The forces touting gun control known as the The Brady Bunch included government and groups much akin to those on the Human Earth, much like the Brady Gun Control Campaign. It claimed a great victory, when honest citizens could no longer hold or own weapons by which to defend themselves. The entire gun control argument was based on the government dispensing doctored statistics to show how crime was decreasing, when in fact it had skyrocketed. The citizens knew the crime rate was escalating because they were not protected like the Pig and Hyena Elites. Either way, the governments of Pig Land and Hyena Land were ecstatic about the gun control since they knew there now remained no existing threat of resistance to their diabolical control over all the other animals!

The Elders of Pig land and Hyena Land, known as the keepers of the wisdom and defenders of Nature, just as in the Native American and aboriginal cultures, shuddered as they contemplated just how disconcerting the situation became as the government assumed even more totalitarian control of the citizens through electronic surveillance. This further stifled dissent against the governments to a point it became perilously dangerous to say anything critical of the governments, no matter how small and insignificant the comment might be. James body shuddered with a cold chill as he recognized a distinct parallel to the animals' plight and the governments in Cuba, North Korea, China and other Communist hell-based utopias!

With things growing close to an ultimate and total control of the people, James' comment was not just a proclamation, but the reality that any dissent directed toward the government meant citizens would be immediately arrested. They would be left to rot in a jail cell for many years, usually without even a trial, with the intent to save the state the expense and time of having a trial.

All James could muster in response was, "Guantanamo, Guantanamo, Guantanamo! What about the myriad enemy combatants held indefinitely without a trial in a legitimate court of law? If you delay the trial long enough they will die in jail! How is this utopia, let alone paradise?"

"This should be truly the embarrassment of my people, in my third-dimension Earth! Aside from this, there are too many civilians in my country convicted of crimes they have never committed! If I were a benevolent King, I would never allow this in my kingdom!"

Waiting for James to finish his diatribe before responding, Ann retorted, *Well, James, you are a Leo in your Vedic Astrology chart and since the Lion denotes Leo, the King of the jungle, you might well make a good benevolent King, hahahaha!*

Anyway, by now, both animal populaces in Pig Land and Hyena Land were entrapped in the noose of government control; tightly fixed about their throats, since being made completely defenseless without their guns! In stark contradistinction to the repression and fear created by gun control in Pig Land and Hyena Land, in the Heaven on Earth of Natural Land, and in the fourth and fifth-dimension, all weapons and munitions had been banned for not only private citizens, but the nominal governments as well! This made sense to James, as he knew only a multilateral ban is the only gun control scenario that works out well for the populace at large!

In Natural Land it was fervently believed there must be a complete absence of guns for everyone and every entity. This concept was not only believed but understood en mass; anyone who thought otherwise was considered to be as deeply confused as Dr. Pangloss in Voltaire's book, *Candide,* wherein Pangloss, often mentioned "this is the best of all possible worlds" and attempted to indoctrinate young Candide with a sense of optimism. However, in Voltaire's work, he writes of an abrupt cessation of the lifestyle, followed by Candide's slow, painful disillusionment—to witness and experience the great hardships in the world. Need we also mention Pollyanna's indoctrination by her father to always play the glad game?

In the end, optimism is a great and valued personality trait, yet one should never say something is good when their life is about to be extinguished or they are strangled by overt control. That was the real possibility facing the animals of Pig Land and Hyena Land, in a figurative sense, at the very least.

Anyway, as was mentioned earlier, eventually the libertarian Earth animals of Natural Land would intervene to save their enslaved counterparts in the Communist infested subdivided dimensions on Earth! One might consider this feat to be impossible; however, the creativity and the mind power of the Natural Land animals would prove to be far more powerful... no, actually vastly more powerful than any weapon! They would also take advantage of their wisdom and awareness of the value of the increasing heat from the Sun, the dimensional uplifting there from, and the morphic resonance from parallel and higher dimensional civilizations—to aid them in their mission—so there would be receptive mental attitudes colored with an assertiveness toward uprising and rebellion!

Since James compared the lethargy on his third dimension Earth, he also pondered when and where these attitudes of rebellion might manifest. Ann wondered much the same, as she clearly shared her thoughts with James, *I wonder too, mon amour!*

CHAPTER FIVE

More Jive
and
Are You Really Saved/Alive?

—————— ⚜ ——————

IT IS KNOWN by most people, Communist governments are atheist in Nature, yet ignoring God is an aberration of Natural Law! To believe there is not a Creator of some sort, or at the minimum, a presence running the show on Planet Earth, could be considered severely short sighted! Yet in the Pig Land and Hyena Land Communist, socialistic governments, a Namor Cilohtac Church and Protesting Churches were allowed to exist—and exist they did with a level of corruption and graft never before experienced on any planet, at least in the case of the Namor Cilohtac Church!

It was interesting, regardless how cosmologically and even in relation to cosmogony, this church was factually incorrect as it claimed the power to act as an intermediary between God and animals—to absolve them of their sins and offer them passageway to Heaven and avoid Hell—if penitents merely confessed their sins and accepted *Cristo Jesus* as their Lord, Master and Savior!

Things grew clearer in James mind, and he slowly elaborated his thoughts to Ann, *It seems to me, a number of things are suspect about these claims. First, what evidence existed that Jesus ever recommended or licensed the Roman Catholic Church in the Human Earth or Cristo in the Namor Cilohtac Church—for the express purpose of being an intermediary for absolution?*

Secondly, the word sin... in the original Hebrew word.... means 'to miss.' it does not mean to commit a wrong, yet it was assumed—actually deliberately perverted—that the word sin equated to evil and wrongness. It is also not surprising that the Bible never attributes moral or cultic evil to God; later human designations formed its definition."

Emotion grabbed hold of James and he shifted from his mental diatribe with Anne, continuing in a passionate voice, "Thirdly, Jesus never talked about people being relegated to Hell! Furthermore, Hell itself was never astro-located or defined as a location in either *The Torah, The Old Testament*, or even *The New Testament!*"

Many of the animals of Pig Land and Hyena Land were echoing James' beliefs and further considered Earth itself might well be Hell, since there was a lot of suffering and fire and brimstone, via volcanic eruptions! Upon hearing and seeing all of this, Ann proffered, *Wow James, your revolutionary fervor seems to be morphically affecting these animals! Are you deliberately working on them, James?*

James laughed as he deftly dodged her, answering Ann's question aloud, "Well, I would never do anything like that, ha-ha, but might know someone really well who would! His name might be Jaime!"

Ann also could not suppress her laughter as she passed her thought back to him, *So... you are telling me without telling me then, huh?*

James arrogantly retorted, "I would never do anything like that... not!"

Everything James had experienced in his long life was that pure teachings and concepts are first embraced and then institutionalized in religions, which then in turn pervert or edit essential teachings of the original teacher and/or source. This then sets the stage to control the subjects of the religion and make them doubt their essential divinity as everything is perverted, twisted and dumbed down. It is at this point they seek the counsel and direction from their church or religion. The lucrative part of this process is when the church/religion claims it can serve as an intermediary to your redemption and salvation.

As James considered all the information running round his head, he stated out loud and thus was inadvertently overheard by some surrounding animals he was surveying, as well as by Ann, "Geez Louise! Who needs any more parasites in their lives? Most people's bodies are already rife with intestinal parasites so who needs religious parasites as well?"

Adding her input Ann shared, *James, you are waxing sardonic and you know your third-dimension Human Earth is infested with parasites that are found everywhere; both the very little ones and the large humankind types!*

Despite the glaring flaws in the Cilohtac doctrine, many animals went for the Church doctrine, hook, line and sinker; this was propitious for the Church, as the leaders could extract tithes—quasi-coerced contributions and donations—from their parishioners. It was not difficult to question whether the tithes were somewhat akin to extortion, in light of the claims of the Namor Cilohtac Church—of it being the only way to salvation and immortal life. In this progression, the Namor Cilohtac Church became immensely wealthy, both legally and through criminal enterprises, as well; all the while never being able to deliver what they promised in the provision of salvation.

Certain Cilohtac parishioner's near-death experiences helped validate the Church's promises were unsubstantiated, where they saw a very different concept of Heaven and Hell than had been described to them by the Cilohtac Church. Their reality was the nonexistence of Hell; there was only Heaven and a type of purgatory, but certainly not the kind of everlasting punishment elicited from the bowels of Hell. With the depth of knowledge given to the animals, came the opportunity to transcend the B.S.; untruths being taught to them! In time, an opportunity was provided whereby the people no longer had to eat the bait of the Cilohtac Church that was ever ready to hook and entrap them, but that would only come upon their eventual emancipation from their governments, as well!

James was aware there is an underlying belief the Roman ruling class wrote *The New Testament*, as a means to control the humans on Earth and make them sources of revenue, similar to the events described in Roman Piso's book, *Piso Christ,* about the origins of Christianity. The manuscript discusses a conspiracy by the well-educated Roman Piso family considered to have written the New Testament, and particularly the Gospels, as a social control mechanism and to enrich themselves as well.

It is more astonishing that possibly other unadulterated and untainted scriptures of Jesus, discussed in William Henry's, *The Secrets of Sion*, known as Gnostic Gospels/Nag Hamadhi documents, were completely ignored and even discredited by both the Roman Catholic and Namor Cilohtac Church. *The Secrets of Sion* represents the culmination of William's unique, long-standing search in Gnostic literature and sacred art to map the path, called the Way of Light, which leads to the gate of heaven. For both James and Ann, it was obvious that the Biblical writers ignoring the texts was intentional... since they neither mentioned the need for salvation, nor delved into a construct of either Hell or sin, yet they did mention evil.

Sadly, as James surveyed everything around him, and as he further intuited the perversions and lack of Godliness and Divinity exhibited by the Namor Cilohtac Church, he learned the misrepresentations did not end there. The Priests in the church were required to be celibate, since it was believed to make them more Godly, being less attached to the flesh and the sensations there from! The lack of forethought that went into the celibacy requirement was appalling as it did little more than make the priests less Godly, since, like their human counterparts, they knew not how to otherwise deal with natural sexual feelings and became pedophillically involved with the Pig Land and Hyena Land children and sexually abused them. The Namor Cilohtac Church even knew about the aberrant behavior, yet chose to ignore such and sweep the facts under the rug to save face over such an ill-designed requirement.

When these animal children, bolstered by the support of other sexually abused victims, had the courage to reveal what happened to them via the priests, most likely since they were tired of being raped and abused, the church denied any such thing could have happened. Eventually, because of a mountain of evidence to the contrary, the Church begrudgingly admitted there were indeed priests who acted inappropriately!

After seeing the synchronicity with what had happened on his third-dimension Human Earth, James was aghast that something like pedophilic priests could happen in yet another place. Just as he was about to think about something more, his deceased wife Ann came to mind again and shortly after her thoughts fell like whispers in James' ear, *I know you are freaked out this pedophilia since your sister was a victim, but it is easier to bear when you are in the ninth-dimension of Heaven, as am I. As traumatic as all this is, you have shared in your book with Dr. Newton, "A Map to Healing and Your Essential Divinity Through Theta Consciousness" how to remove the negative memories and the damage they cause in people's minds.*

James, you owe it to yourself to not get pulled backward since, as you well know, these animals of Pig Land and Hyena Land need a helping hand to extricate themselves from the miasmas and misery of Communism.

"Yes, I know you are correct in your assessments, James replied, yet I might never be able to accept the depravity of all of this, even more so because it was done under the cloak of religious authority! Well, actually it was done under mantle of false and disingenuous religious authority!"

The parents of the Pig Land and Hyena Land children sued the responsible churches in a court of law. Although the families actually received significant monetary judgments from the Church, it is not difficult to perceive the stipend was exceedingly inadequate, even though it came with punitive as well as actual damages, to compensate for the emotional damage the children would have and how it would affect them in their own romantic relationships when they became older. Additionally, the church, because of the large judgments they had to pay for the pedophilic priests' actions, claimed it might have to declare bankruptcy!

In seeing this, James' mind was suddenly filled with passion, and his thoughts reflected his deep emotions, *This is obviously disingenuous!*

Ann finished his thoughts as she continued, *How could any church that owns such obscene amounts of money and property, be even remotely bankrupt? What a truly interesting phenomenon... for a church under the authority of a Communist government allowed to amass odious amounts of money and property from its numerous criminal activities, including money laundering, prostitution, sexual slavery and illegal drug dealing!*

James kept the mental connection with Ann going as he circumspectly added, *Obviously, the Pig Land and Hyena Land governments are getting a large cut of the action/take or none of this would have been allowed to happen through the Namor Cilohtac Church! In any case, there was a severe dereliction of duty by both the church and government authorities to allow any of these things to happen.*

Ann's experience of the corruption and waywardness of the Roman Catholic Church and the Namor Cilohtac Church were gained from the experiences she related in the book, *An Angel Not Perceived.* Even with her angelic origins, Ann saw no redeeming value and guidance in either entity other in the dispensation of fairy tales and the fantasies related to these.

The Protesting Churches, although they were less involved in questionable activities, some more than others, were still culpable of accepting the teaching of the Namor Cilohtac Church, as applied to the accurate dispensing of the teaching of Cristo. The Protesting Churches came into existence primarily to rebel against the corruption of the Cilotac Church orthodoxy! Most notably was the ensuing questionable reliability of the *New Testament* being accurately dispensed and the Protesting Church's failure to account for the editing of the New Testament and for ignoring *The Gnostic Scriptures*, suppressed by the Cilohtac Church. So the Protestants, who believed they were in rebellion against a corrupt Namor Cilohtac Church, did not protest so much as they fervently believed... at least that is how it appeared to James and Ann!

Was the ingenuity of using the name of God and Jesus, as a front for a criminal and disingenuous enterprise not a brilliant maneuver... although diabolical and unethical, to wit? James thought, Eventually, the animals in Pig Land and Hyena Land would demand this Tower of Babel be liquidated and its resources, deceptively accumulated from the masses, be distributed to the very people who were preyed upon via false promises.

Coming around full circle, just how does this sharing of events relate to the totalitarian Communist governments enacted by the Pigs and Hyenas? James shared his perception of this as his thoughts took form, *Directly, this does not relate to the Communist governments. However, it does show all the third-dimension Earths, the human one and the subdivided two animal Earths, operated in a space of great deception; this includes all societal entities, which seek to extort money voluntarily or involuntarily from the Hyena Land and Pig Land animals, whether it was through taxes or false promises of dispensation and an immortal life in Heaven.*

James' passion got the best of him, and his quiet thoughts once again were quite vocal as he loudly exclaimed, "All of this stems from religions so flawed as to never remotely be able to deliver on their promises and in the end, such promises were only made for profit, to generate huge sums of money!"

Our story continues as we wonder, "Could things get worse?" Well actually they could, and did, get worse! Eventually the pendulum would swing back in the opposite direction... by nature's laws, embodied in the laws of Physics, just as it inevitably always does, in the Third Law of Thermodynamics, for every action, there is an equal and opposite reaction! The right and true ways of life and living are always made visible... to be seen, and to follow as is apparent in the Earth of Natural Land. In the fourth and fifth-dimensions, things remained in a middle ground, in relation to the extremes of a pendulum. For one thing, there were no organized religions, nor the abuses of power and promises that always seem to accompany them. Secondly, the only religion, per se, which the animals needed, was that of Nature and the Natural Laws that are always evident and available to observe via how the forces of Nature operate! These laws are easy to understand, albeit, more difficult to follow when Communists are in control and distort the perfect pictures, templates and guidelines of Nature and Natural Law, deduced and distilled therein by the animals of Natural Land. This was done not in a constitution but passed down through an oral tradition, by the Elders... wise men... wise women.... to the newer souls within their society.

First: All resources are and will be shared, regardless of the tree, plant or animal species involved; no one will be allowed to hoard and monopolize resources.

Second: Everything is done from a standpoint of sustainability, meaning things are used and consumed only as much as they can be replaced and regenerated and nothing is done or used that becomes or causes any type of pollution or environmental degradation (an example of this would be harvesting Timber Bamboo and Hemp in *lieu* of timber from trees);

From James' and Ann's knowledge of these matters, each is evidenced by Pantheism, Zeitgeist, *Thrive* (the documentary) and *Avatar* (the movie), *Beyond the Mists of Time: When Trees Ruled the Earth* (the book*)*, and well-documented in the writings of English philosophers such as John Locke and Thomas Hobbes, and the American Trancendalists including Ralph Waldo Emerson, Walt Whitman, John Whittier and Henry David Thoreau in his book, *On Walden Pond*; who are the standard bearers both historical and current.

Third: Introducing industrialization and metropolitan development to cities is to be avoided at all costs or undertaken with very tight and controlled parameters, so as to defile Nature as little as possible, and to mitigate any wounds man inflicts on its Mother

Earth, with any and all restoration, as necessary to mitigate any and all damage thereto!

Thus, with these clear directives as a backdrop, and with the influence of morphic resonance, a new direction was now available for the third-dimension subdivisions of Earth, controlled by the Pig and Hyena Elites. What then became necessary was for the animals to start questioning those in control so there would be movement back to liberty and freedom, and sustainability! Was this on the horizon? James and Ann fervently hoped so!

CHAPTER SIX

Looking For A Fix

———— ⚬✦⚬ ————

THE FORCES OF repression on the third-dimension Earth controlled by the Pigs Elites in Pig Land and the Hyena Elites in Hyena Land created a scenario where everything would implode, as layer after of layer of oppressive control was stacked upon the populace! But before this would happen, a few more layers—one huge one in particular—would be heaped upon the Proletariat!

A constant stream of reports surfaced, each regaling the dysfunctional lives of celebrities, be they singers or actors or even politicians modeled upon the "misdirection play" from the Earth's American football, where the opposing team is made to believe a runner is taking off in one direction, through a fake play, but then giving the ball to another runner going a different direction. About this James opined "How keenly those in control occupy the minds of the subservient animals, with a constant stream of inane entertainment and babble that deflects them away from perceiving just how bad their lives were successively becoming, day after day!"

Similar to the third dimension Human Earth's publications such as *The Inquirer* and TV shows like *Entertainment Tonight,* the media constantly dispensed reel after reel of celebrity pabulum and the inane travails of actors, athletes, singers and politicians

As though the level of control having been exercised thus far was not sufficient, James and Ann sensed another disconcerting factor in the Pig/Hyena Earths... a rather intense effort by the governments to control even the thoughts and values of the animals. This was done through legal coercion via the passing of hate crimes laws, which were supposedly related to a new perspective of political correctness. If an animal's personal thoughts deviated from those foisted upon them by the Communist Pig or Hyena governments, whether it be about homosexuality, transgender issues, gender equality, or related to racial matters, the offending party was not only deemed politically incorrect, but also found guilty of committing hate crimes, which were punishable by imprisonment! So insults, questionable slang, or anything denigrating to anyone or anything, pretty much would mean myriad animals would wind up in prison, even if the supposed transgression was done without bullying or accompanied with genuine humor!

During James' and Ann's mental discourse on this matter, they concluded after some deliberation, it was not that anyone should be prejudiced against minorities, etc.; rather just the sheer volume of onerous dictates to compel citizens to think in a certain manner, squelched individualism, and installed state control in its place—the ultimate repression! The state seemed determined to "mold" people's thoughts and literally control them, and considering how dysfunctional and hypocritical the Pig and Hyena Elites were, as participants in a Circus of the Cukoobirds, all of this was amusing while concurrently being blatantly unjust! For James, this hit "to close to home" as he had come to despise the dictates of "political correctness" that had become the incessant agenda on his Earth homeland, with anyone daring to defy the coercion of '"political correctness" being pilloried in the media outlets and even prosecuted for so called "hate crimes." The tide pushing this theoretical political correctness" was relentless and overwhelming.

Yet another distressing issue involved how the Pig and Hyena governments were able to create civil unrest through black operations, false flag operations, or covert operations, which were funded off the books by offending Pig Land and Hyena Land governments. The twist here was although the events were government-funded operations they were far too frequently blamed on so called "terrorists," similar to the actions of earth humans such as Muslim jihadists or patriot organizations.

Many of these "black ops" were known to a very few animals... having been undertaken by private mercenary groups, similar to the Craft Group—an American group of privately held companies with a stronghold in 90 countries— and the ability to create certain false flag operations, deemed deft and deadly, to wit! They left a trail of death in their wake and yet were able to flee the scene of a "terrorist attack" undetected and not apprehended. James had heard of so many scenarios regarding these activities that he always disregarded any report ascribing these terror scenes as the work of Muslim jihadists and citizen domestic terrorists in his third dimension Human Earth. He just could not ignore the evidence, though in many ways, he would have rather not even have to make the realization his own government had *de facto* declared war against its own people. James trembled emotionally as he reflected, *It is a bitter pill to swallow when our own government considers us to be expendable.*

This deceptive exercise of power and control was bad enough in and of itself yet what was worse was the loss of civil liberties; akin to actions experienced by their human counterparts when rights were completely stripped, through legislation such as The Patriot Act, The Homeland Security

Act (HSA) and the National Defense Authorization Act (NDAA), for which the animals actually clamored so they could be protected from the so called terrorists! After this plethora of restricted civil liberties, citizen communication of any and all types were under constant surveillance, having the effect of animals and their human counterparts being virtually imprisoned, at least figuratively, if not literally... and if one thought long and hard—far more literally than figuratively!

Pondering this, James deduced, *Considering the terrorists were the governments themselves, at least in a conspiratorial sense—the animals have really been set up on this one, and so have my human compatriots.*

Intuiting James' thoughts, Ann added, *Well, I am reading your mind James and if a full, open, and accurate appraisal of this situation is undertaken, I can only say you are correct, more correct and the most correct.*

Again, James detected a morphic resonance between the third-dimension Human Earth and the subdivided dimensions of Pig Land and Hyena Land. For James, it did not matter in which dimension change occurred first but more that there were cause and effect interferences bleeding through from one dimension to another, as it were. In this specific case the word "bleeding" has a heightened significance, since many animals and people are injured and killed in these faux terrorist attacks.

Need it be said that in the end, these black ops were created to justify the draconian laws and constant citizen surveillance? As diabolical as these actions were, one rather had to admire the way things were crafted to obfuscate their true purpose and intention! Interestingly enough, the terrorist attacks still continued after the legislation to prevent such it was passed so the Hyena and Pig Elites/governments "had their cake and ate it too!" The animals did not eat cake or anything even nearly as tasty, however; their fare was actually more like the grass similar to what the people of North Korea eat! James was reflecting that the Elite Pigs and Hyenas were already fat enough, without eating more cake or even any other food, for that matter.

Unfortunately, all that thus far had transpired was "small potatoes" compared to what was about to occur. The Hyena Land government and the Pig Land governments had for a long time held a strong disagreement about the allocation of water resources; nothing addressed during informal or formal negotiations led to any resolution of the matter. So in a covert military operation, in the middle of negotiations, the Hyena Land military command directed a covert attack upon the seat of the Pig Land government. The Pigs repelled this attack by the use of Sarin nerve gas, as some Hyena Land dissident informants tipped them off about the attack! As another of life's stark ironies, the gas quickly killed the Hyena invaders but also killed many of the Pig Land animal citizens—all innocent victims of the reckless and "damn the consequences" attitude of government officials. The very animals they were pledged to protect were nevertheless killed anyway.

In retaliation, the Pig Land military struck back with a counter covert attack upon the Hyena seat of government. The Hyena Elites, suspecting retaliation, were ready for the Pig assault and released a virulent, manmade virus, which summarily killed the Pig invaders, but also killed many of the animals under the control of the Hyena government. You would think this might be the end of these hostilities yet that rarely happens in the throes of war, were there are almost always attacks and counteracts in a series of hostile exploits. Both sides were getting ready to launch a nuclear missile attack against their enemy.

The Natural Land animals in the parallel, fourth and fifth-dimension Earth, got wind of the impending nuclear holocaust, again due to morphic resonance and the intuitional perception of their nominal elder leader, Enoch. They used high tech space ships, equipped with electromagnetic pulse (EMP), and laser weapons to neutralize the nuclear missiles on both sides of this conflict, by traveling through an inter dimensional worm hole! It was agreed by Enoch, with the consensus of animals in Natural Land, they simply could not allow a nuclear war, as it would affect the space-time continuum and possibly pull them back into the third-dimension. What must be done must! Not one of them wanted any part of the limitations of the third-dimension, which they often referred to as the turd-dimension. Nobody in Natural Land was eager to go backwards dimensionally with the inherent limitations that caused everything to be harder to achieve, not to mention, it made for bodies far more inclined to deterioration.

They were equally concerned about the effects of radioactive pollution, as they had knowledge that the radiation could move through the energy membranes... separating the dimensions and spread nuclear radiation elsewhere! The further consideration was that any civilization that had to use nuclear weapons, were found to be immature and childlike and in need supervision and direction, just as children need attention and counseling in their youth! From James and Ann's detached observer status, there could be nothing said to contradict this assessment, and each took seriously the possibility of a huge nuclear event about to occur.

In fact, James and Ann considered the assessment of the Pig Land and Hyena Land governments by Enoch and his compatriots to be rather restrained. They saw things in a harsher perspective, such as putting Pig Land and Hyena Land in a protectorate status, where the ability of the Pig and Hyena Elites to direct their governments was severely limited, in a receivership of sorts. James also expressed his feelings on the matter, "It would seem my own third-dimension Earth has many countries that are in need of strict supervision and receivership, as well, ha-ha!"

Luckily all citizen animals of Pig Land and Hyena Land were spared the horrors and deaths from a nuclear war. Some of these animals later thought, however, they would perhaps have been better dead than alive. The feeling prevailed, even if it were a slow death from radiation poisoning, since death was thought to be a preferable alternative to the hellish existence in a totalitarian Communist nightmare, in which they found themselves currently enveloped.

Such a frightening death wish alternative came in light of the circumstances where both the Pig and Hyena Elite governments decided that henceforth, the animals would be charged for the very air they breathed, furthering the animal's sense of desperation. For virtually all the animals, this was "the last straw!" They were already previously charged for what had been free food and water, followed by space rent and now... air became just another part of an obvious pay for everything scheme! James had many thoughts about viewing this, and put forth a solution, which he had learned and felt confident enough to share out loud, "These animals need to learn to attain the breathless state of Samadhi, preceded by the breathing meditation of Kriya Kundalini Pranayam."

Ann's reflected thoughts presented her assent, *I agree, Mr. Smarty Pants, James, and you need to remember who was the insistent angelic presence who pushed you into learning the Pranayam breathing meditation that liberates both our bodies and our minds."*

James just heartily laughed at Ann's proclamation and nodded his head up and down in agreement.

Shortly thereafter, low and behold! James and Ann saw there were a number of animal citizens who seemed to have attained a state of breathlessness in Samadhi shortly after

James' and Ann's comments, and even some of them were Breatharians, so they did not need to eat either. The Breatharians seemed to have learned how to create energy to run their bodies, just as the trees had been doing for billions of years using photosynthesis to create chlorophyll, taking sunlight and the interaction of the water in their bodies— creating a photosynthesis that resulted in an electromagnetic form of energy—essentially Prana/Chi/God life force

Both of these things—the breathless state of Samadhi and Breathairianism—were rare but they did occur. Yet even to these particular groups of animals, this did not matter, because the animals of Pig Land and Hyena Land, en masse, had reached their breaking point! There was a strong acrimony toward the governments and a building anxiety, which was growing close to exploding... much akin to a lid about to be blown off a pressure cooker.

There were many casualties from the war, on both sides of the conflict, with many dead and wounded soldiers, as well as citizens. The soldiers that were wounded would have been better off dying, considering the very governments that had promised to care for them if they were injured, conveniently forgot the promises and told the soldiers most of their PTSD problems were psychosomatic in origin, and took a position the mental-related problems were not covered under the standard military provisions for health and wellness.

Regardless the truth to these statements, the soldiers were so emotionally devastated from seeing their fellow soldiers injured and killed, they were not functional as inhabitants on Pig Land and Hyena Land, and forced to live in a state of constant depression, arguing, and engaging in violence toward their wives or husbands and children. Unfortunately, over a period of time, the effects of the battlefield trauma figuratively sent out long tentacles of trauma, drama and ill health that also affected non-battlefield participants.

Another travesty was seen in the many soldiers who had limbs that had been amputated and it took a private organization, known as The Warrior Wounded Project, to undertake the task of getting prosthetic limbs for the soldiers; a task purported to have been provided by the governments who simply never fulfilled their commitment to doing such. James could feel the malodorous similarities to what happened on his planet relative to PSTD, among other things, and the help from the private Wounded Warrior Project, filling the needs of the soldiers ignored by the scofflaw governments. Ann shared her thoughts on the matter with James, *It is really too dangerous to be a soldier, even if on the winning side, since there is little real guarantee your injuries will be taken care of, despite the protestations of governments to the contrary.*

James could do little more than his eyebrows in assent.

These soldiers, having seen the horrors of war, started a movement to prevent any more wars from every being concocted; they coined the undertaking NOMOWO (No More War). It is not difficult to imagine the dismay of those soldiers who suffered so much when they learned how the international banking cartel made a lot of money from any war in which they were combatants, through the underhanded banks loaning money to both sides in the conflict. What really solidified this movement were the soldiers in the third-dimension Human Earth, during World War II; they discovered the international bankers who funded the war efforts of the so-called enemy of Nazi Germany and the Allies at the same time. Further, they learned Prescott Bush, father of President George Bush, was the delivery conduit for the war funds to the Nazis. All of this infuriated the soldiers and made them more determined to end the idiocy and destructiveness of war. How they learned of the World War II situation is hard to ascertain, but both Ann and James sent out incessant telepathic messages about the situation and there perhaps was a morphic resonance or telepathic connection in relation to the events... they just could not determine this for sure.

There was another affliction thrust again, upon the animals in both Pig and Hyena Land. Once again, mysterious things started happening in the skies, akin to the contrails left by the exhaust from jet engines. The governments of Pig Land and Hyena Land had decided to spray the deadly aerosols into the atmosphere again. Jet planes were used to lay down these trails, but they were chemical aerosols comprised of coal ash, which contained aluminum oxide, barium oxide and strontium 90, which is a radioactive isotope of strontium produced by nuclear fission, with a half-life of 28.8 years. Unlike contrails, which quickly dissolve, the chemtrails aerosol would slowly spread out in the skies, eventually creating a haze from the many trails, which were present most of the time. So the mounting illnesses previously mentioned, began to mount in such numbers among the animals that there were not enough medical facilities to treat them, and caused many people to die, untreated. James was aware of this same thing occurring in his third-dimension Human Earth, at least in regard to people being made sick from toxic atmospheric chemicals.

In Pig Land, the animals once again asked their LARD Legislators what was being sprayed into the skies and they were given a consistently disingenuous response, as was used before, "Oh, it is really nothing more than contrails." Once in a while, a weatherman on the nightly news would talk about the aerosols being some kind of chaff, used in military exercises to evade radar detection. Yet as the animals started experiencing respiratory problems—and aluminum, barium and strontium 90 was detected in their water and milk—the animals accepted the harsh reality: their government was deceiving them.

As with James, Ann had done a lot of research on the issue of how we incarnate on Earth and now with her perspective from heaven... she had done a lot of research into the reality of these chemical aerosols in his Earth and knew there were at least three reasons for this campaign of chemical aerosols, as James had previously mentioned:

One: To mitigate a global warming trend, blamed on carbon emissions from human industrial activity and motor vehicles, wherein the haze in the sky cooled the Earth to some extent... and counteracting a believed "greenhouse effect," more attributable to the Sun combusting at a higher temperature due to being surrounded by a cloud of hydrogen.

Another: To control weather patterns, creating more rain in some places and less in other locales, among other weather phenomena.

Still Another: A synthetic ionosphere was created, facilitating the dispersal of electronic signals carrying brainwashing and propaganda programs to control people in a desired manner, making them more compliant and unconcerned about the fact they were being bombarded with myriad toxins dispersed in the atmosphere.

Finally: A weapon-ization of the atmosphere making it possible to more easily facilitate the use of EMP (electromagnetic pulse) weapons, various particle beam weapons, and other things related thereto.

In James' Human Earth dimension, Ann could see the Sun was in an area of its orbit, inhabited by excess hydrogen from an exploded star, which caused the Sun to combust with more intensity and was vastly more responsible for global warming than the promoted carbon emission-greenhouse gas theory. Ann and James further considered the weather on his Earth was much more extreme than before the skies were flooded with toxic aerosols. As to the brainwashing and propaganda programs being broadcast... this was hard to prove, but for sure the visual media outlets in his Earth were certainly rife with subliminal pictures that could be used to modify and direct the behavior of citizens. As to the weapon-ization of the atmosphere—again, this was harder to prove than the type of activities, which were shared by people who had worked on the development of these weapons, and which were made off the record.

Literally every animal under the control of the totalitarian, Communist government was now ready for a revolution; everyone was talking about the possibility, even though it was against the laws that had been passed and even if this meant a violent rebellion, so be it! The bigger question was whether things would get down and be really nasty or whether there be a measured response by the desperate and oppressed animals. At this point in time, neither James nor Ann knew how things would play out, even though they were immersed in the trail of events. But for sure, a "breaking point" had been reached and the animals were ready to rebel and throw off their oppressors.

CHAPTER SEVEN

Way Past Time
to Return to Heaven

————— ~⸙~ —————

BEFORE WE GET to the "last straw" that finally thrust the animals in a rebellion against their Pig and Hyena Communist oppressors, an intervening situation needs to be discussed. There was a country, known as Learsi... a well-known Socialist/Communist religious state, in a subdivided Earth dimension of Pig Land and Hyena Land. Founded by the Pig Elites, Learsi was a very small country, yet it was with great power and influence over the events on this subdivided third-dimension Earth, to wit! The Elitist Pigs therein, claimed they were "the chosen people of God!" These claims of being the chosen people were contained in their religious book, *The Harot*, which supposedly was written by God.

However, the God being referred to, King Line, a.k.a., Enil, was really a person from an extraterrestrial planet, Uribin, a.k.a., Nibiru. Yet virtually none of the animals in Learsi really understood the distinction between God, the Creator and the more evolved, ET animals that seemed to have Godlike qualities—but were not in fact God. These demi-gods had super powers... physical, psychic and mental. There was also another book they followed known as the *Dumlat,* and said book considered all other religions and races as inferior to the people of Learsi. The Learsi Elites used a term, Muyog, to describe all non-Learsi animals and this meant livestock that needed to be herded. As James and Ann viewed what transpired, they shared simultaneous thoughts as they laughed in disbelief... *This sure seems similar to how many people have described as what would be attributed to Israel but we are not really sure if this is true! It sounds rather harsh!*

There was a sect among the people of Learsi, known as Tsinoizs who took the teachings of *The Harot*, disregarded the teachings of love and compassion therein, and created yet another repressive and jingoistic, war-like government. This government attacked and subjugated its nation's neighbors, through direct attacks and stealth black operations, deluded as they were, in the name of God, even though that God had issued a commandment, "Thou shalt not kill!" It was most ironic, these Pigs, who asserted a superior status to all other animals, would eventually be killed and eaten themselves, even though one of the laws in their religious text, *The Harot,* forbade the eating of pork... and for James and Ann, the irony of it all was very difficult to ignore.

The undoing of Learsi would ultimately be a rebellion by a group of animals, Baras, who were displaced from a land they had occupied and ruled for several millennia. When the country Learsi was created, the Baras were relegated to an inferior status in Learsi and there was a subtle campaign of genocide against them. They were relocated into reservations, similar to large prisons, after which the Learsi military forces wrought more destruction by bombing the infrastructure... including hospitals, sewage treatment plants, water supplies and even residences. Subsequently, the increasing oppression would lead to a violent overthrow of the Pig Elites in Learsi, and in a very short period of time.

Such irony was impossible for James and Ann to overlook and in their thoughts simultaneously exclaimed, *This sure sounds like the scourge of Zionism, yet how many Jews would ever be able to accept and digest this!*

James then further clarified his feelings as he proclaimed, "But it is a very few of these Jews, a sect and cult, known as Zionists, that have created the attitudes of Jewish superiority over all other peoples and nations. So we must be careful not to paint things with a broad stroke and impute these attitudes to all Israelis or Jews in general."

Another event which added fuel to the fire, was the feeling the banking systems installed by the Pig families— similar to the Human third-dimension Earth Federal Reserve Bank, of Rockefeller, Rothschild, Warburg, Mellon, Morgan and Schwab—was only beneficial for the Elites. In Pig Land, Hyena Land, and Learsi, a system of fractionalized banking was created, issuing money into circulation from their so-called federal bank. The Reserve Federal, which was really private, was backed with nothing of inherent value like gold or silver! This *de facto* Ponzi scheme served to allow the respective governments to spend more money than they collected from taxes and fees, and engage in deficit spending.

Since there was not a lot of money in circulation, at first there was not a huge problem with the deficit spending by the government. However, as more money was created—and it was printed everyday in larger amounts—the inflationary effect was severely felt, and as increasing amounts of money was printed without serious consideration and brazenly put into circulation, it became commensurately less valuable. This meant with each successive day, the same amount of money earned by the animals bought a reduced amount of goods and services. Everything was modeled on the Human Earth Ponzi scheme known as the Federal Reserve Bank, which had absolutely no vestiges of being federal, other than the inclusion of the word, federal, in its moniker.

As James and Ann considered the monetary issues, it was depressing to see other countries also scammed by a fractionalized banking system. Thereby, the animals were bamboozled into believing their governments controlled the money when that in fact was untrue. This was all too well known to James since the fraud by these private banks with their vapor currency and masquerading as federal banks is one of the great frauds of twentieth and twenty-first century human history.

The reason more money had to be put into circulation was predicated by the governments of Pig Land and Hyena Land and Learsi spending increased amounts of money, a lot of which was wasted on wars, black operations and false flag operations, and allowed for vast amounts of money to be allocated to the very government officials and legislators who had developed a proclivity to live their lives in an opulent manner. In contrast to the other animals, the resultant spending on lavish lifestyles of the Pig and Hyena elite, legislators and government officials, led to increasing pain and poverty heaped upon the Proletariat animal populace and a vast energy field of resentment... a morphic field that was pervasive throughout the populaces! This discontent and rebellion spread like a virulent disease.

Finally... enough was enough! Over time, with each new control mechanism put in place, the animals felt the effects of, and recognized in them, the onerous accumulation thereof: virtually no personal freedom, being charged for food, water and air, and being tied to money that pulled all but the Pig, Hyena and Learsi Elites into poverty. Something had to give because as the animals stress increased, it brought them closer to a breaking point and the dying point, as well!

As was previously mentioned, many of the animals practiced meditation, Kriya Kundalini Yoga; and Tai Chi Chuan "Standing Meditation." Even though such activities were outlawed in Pig and Hyena governments via legislation and bureaucratic decrees, it was very fortuitous that many of the animals ignored these laws. Fortunately for the animals of Pig Land, Hyena Land, and Learsi, the practices of meditation, Yoga and Tai Chi, became a lifesaver of sorts, and ultimately developed the animals' intuition and their connection to their Creator/God—certainly something they did not get from the Protesting, Hsiwej and Nomar Cilohtac Churches, who served up their usual fare of salvation in an afterlife, but were devoid of any solutions for pressing problems in the here and now!

The animals that meditated, in conjunction with their inner guidance and with help from the animals of the fourth and fifth-dimension of Natural Land, fomented a revolution. Said revolution was really a no loss situation for the animals since their lives were so controlled and their freedom's so quashed that the feeling prevailed... there was little remaining worth living for above and beyond the potential promise of freedom! Whether an animal existed in a physical prison or not, in the realm of being controlled... their lives outside of prison felt much the same as though they resided inside.

Eventually, in light of this *nothing-to-lose* scenario, the first steps of the revolution were brought to fruition. With help from sympathetic Pigs and Hyenas and Learsi animals, within the Pig and Hyena controlled governments and in Learsi— those who were repulsed by the oppressive totalitarian government enacted on their Pig and Hyena and Learsi brothers, sisters, and compatriots, who were forced to live in squalor and poverty—the Proletariat started a work strike, wherein most of the animals refused to work any longer in dead end jobs! The Communist order and controlled machine was brought to a grinding halt in short order. Even the electrical grid was shut down because the workers in the plants refused to staff or run them.

Immediately, the Pig and Hyena and Learsi Elites were freaked out, because their privileged and opulent life styles were being threatened. How were they going to be able to have their lavish parties with no caterers and no lighting or power... no musicians or entertainment? The Elites started to arrest and imprison the protesters, but they soon realized they did not have enough jail space to imprison the mass numbers. The next plan of attack was to curtail the selling of food through government and black market sources, using scare tactic to force the protesting animals into going back to work. Unfortunately for them, the animals were so pissed off they really didn't care since living in a "Hell on Earth" had little hope attached to it. Because of the work strike, the Elites finally started to feel the same pain and uncertainty in their lives as their animal subjects. The Pig and Hyena, and Learsi Elites, started to experience the fear they had for so long dispensed to the Proletariat; quite the shift as the populace started to acquire the confidence formerly exuded only by the Elites.

What really aided and allowed this revolution to proceed was the fact that the fourth and fifth-dimension Earth animals of Natural Land used their highly developed psychic abilities and psychotronic devices to confuse and paralyze the Pig and Hyena government officials, and armies and police. They also used the power of focused electromagnetic energy pulses (EMP's) with aspects of a "death ray," that served to confuse, demoralize, and even physically injure the Pig, Hyena and Learsi Elites. The EMP's were easily directed specifically at the offenders, through the use of their pictures on the psychotronic/radionic machine plates!

As amazing and effective as this was, the mental and psychotronic/radionic attacks were conjunct with a type of mind control, which was as effective, if not more so, than using weapons... without all the gore and indiscriminate damage from bullets, bombs and grenades! The animals of Natural Land detected that their compatriots in parallel Earth dimensions were in duress, through the morphic resonance fields of thought they detected through their psychic powers: intuition, clairvoyance (seeing), clairaudience (hearing), and clairsentience (feeling). Some of the animals of Pig Land, Hyena Land and Learsi Land, likewise, knew the animals of Natural Land would be coming to aid them, so it took very little time before the Pig and Hyena Land and Learis governments began to crumble... and their leaders attempted to flee to underground safe havens they had previously created for the eventuality of mass civil unrest and nuclear wars.

These safe havens created by the Elites reminded James of the similar sheltered havens created by his U.S. government throughout the U.S.—in such places as Sandia Mountain, Stapleton International Airport in Denver, Harper's Ferry, West Virginia and many other places connected together with underground tunnels and transportation.

Most unfortunate for the Pig and Hyena and Learis Elites: they were easily found in the underground havens because the animals that constructed the fortifications knew where they were and how to circumvent the security measures to protect them. All of the Elites were rounded up for their crimes against other animals, and many were beheaded via guillotines that were constructed, since there were few weapons available by which to shoot the Elite Pigs, Hyenas and Tsinoizs of Learsi. It was highly ironic... the very gun control enacted by the Pigs and Hyenas to protect them from the Proletariat, wound up providing them with a vastly more gruesome death, in the binds of the guillotine.

When James and Ann reviewed the equivalent of the events on James' third-dimension Human Earth, they saw some that were very similar to what transpired in "the river of blood" during the French Revolution! Ann then pointed out to

James, *Sometimes, irony takes on a tone of being very twisted, such as what transpired when the Pig Land and Learis laws, which forbade the consumption of pork, was ignored and some of the animal protestors or revolutionaries ate the beheaded Pigs. After all James, the animals were very hungry!*

James then replied in that mind-filled way in which he now communicated with Ann, *Well, considering the onerous and greedy morphic vibrations contained in those Pigs, we both know there will be little benefit, and a lot of detriment, from eating flawed and diseased souls.*

In fact, the fourth and fifth-dimension animals of Natural Land, who "traveled" to the subdivided third-dimension Earth of animals, tried to counsel their brethren about the dangers of consuming pork. They told the animals, "Pork is a very unclean meat, full of parasites and worms, and even more, the energy from these unevolved Pigs and Hyenas, devoid of the most basic love and spiritual values will negatively affect and debase you!"

In light of all of this, Ann then shared with James, *Negative results stem from negative actions and when anyone consumes a food containing the unclean, they must know they are subject to any negativity emanating there from.*

Unfortunately, the animals that ignored the caveats related to eating the tainted pork suffered the expected fate there from and the advice and prophesy of the evolved Natural Land animals proved quite prescient! The wayward animals became seriously ill; many of them died. This was probably propitious for them, as mean as this sounds, since the animals that survived seemed trapped in the negative energy of the pigs they ate, which resulted in the need to go through a major ordeal to rid themselves of the unevolved Pig vibes—by smudging themselves with sage smoke—to remove negative vibrations from the Pigs and Tsinoizs. The smudging process was the easiest step to remove the negative energy. Further methods required reciting *The 72 Names God*, and using therapy that involved mind reprogramming such as Theta Consciousness Healing and Reprogramming, as discussed in the publication, *A Map to Healing and Your Essential Divinity Through Theta Consciousness*.

Upon seeing the results of meat consumption, the animals realized eating meat had too many negative effects; exactly the sentiments and counsel expressed to them by the Natural Land animals of the fourth and fifth-dimension. The Natural Land animals never ate the flesh of another being and were commensurately benefited thereby, because their bodies were free from parasite, worms, or the negative energies of death the eaten animals projected into their bodies just before and during the process of their demise!

Once the existing governments of Pig Land, Hyena Land and Learis were in deep disarray, it was easy to dismantle the oppressive, totalitarian Communist governments, erected by the Pigs and Hyenas and Tsinoizs. In its place stood a sort Libertarian government—a more natural order of things, based on Nature and Natural Law, with aspects of Anarchy (literally meaning no government) contained therein.

"Ah!" declared James. "How exciting to see the new order replace the insane and bizarre experiment foisted upon the populaces who had to experience totalitarian Communism-Socialism... not to mention the plethora of evils and dysfunction that emanated there from! "

The formerly enslaved animals were profusely happy for the help from the fourth-fifth-dimension compatriots from Natural Land. In the course of a conversation, the nominal Elder leader of the Pig Land animals, Farmer John, asked the nominal leader, Enoch, of the fourth-fifth-dimension Natural Land animals, "Just why did you help us? This really is not your problem! Don't get me wrong, I don't even know if we could have over thrown our nefarious Communist government without your help, and we appreciate it much more than you can imagine!"

Farmer John was surprised by the response from the Natural Land animal Elder, Enoch, "Actually, what was happening in your third-dimension Earth was affecting us and in a negative fashion, undoubtedly!

Enoch continued, "The answer is quite simple. You see, it has been scientifically proven in Quantum Mechanics; everything is interrelated—not only on your dimension, between animals, trees, plants and humans—but also myriad parallel and higher dimensions! As you are affected, so we are too; as you evolve, so do we evolve in kind. If you get pulled backward, so do we! This is something that has always been known in the Animal Kingdom and what happened in your world was a bizarre aberration, a Kafkaesque experiment that never leads to anything good, despite the promises filled with flatulence promoting the Communist-socialist idiocy! That idiocy is manifest in the Communist miasma that claims all animals are equal and interconnected and yet winds up creating classes of animals, where some are more than equal and far more privileged than the Proletariat."

Enoch elaborated in more detail as he exclaimed, "You intuitively knew how things are supposed to be, in a natural balance manifested as Paradise and perfection, so now you must be ever-vigilant against the hollow and mispercepted promises of Pigs, Hyenas or Tsinoizs or any other animal or human. I can assure you they will try this same nightmarish, discombobulated, dysfunctional government again, until you teach and educate them how things work in Nature and the Natural Law that naturally follows there from. Therein are the keys to your future liberty, happiness and prosperity. It is apparent you have animals with genetic defects in that they have not had the memories of how Nature and Natural Law operate embedded in their DNA; hence, they don't' "get it" and thus, do not understand the perfect operating system within Nature, itself!"

Enoch left Farmer John with a lot to consider from what he had shared. As he replied to Enoch, Farmer John's thoughts began to form, *We certainly have a lot to do and it all seems kind of overwhelming.*

Almost immediately, Enoch smiled as he responded with his own thoughts, *Well, yes, you do have a lot to do, but really you simply need to go back to the old ways of doing things that you did before the Communist intrusion into your lives. It is truly that simple... and virtually everyone, other than the Pig, Hyena, and Tsinoizs Elites, is on board to continue supporting you so there will be a lot of shoulders available to make this happen.*

After a few moments of reflection, Enoch shared more wisdom. "After you get your own society in order, you can help the third-dimension Humans turn their things around, just as we in Natural Land have helped you. The Humans are mired in repressive and totalitarian Communist governments, even though many of them are not generally considered such. The populace there is basically clueless about the reality of their situation, so we need your help to help them. A time will come when the Humans will rebel against the repressive and nefarious governments in which they are currently enmeshed."

Enoch continued to elaborate on things he deemed to be very important for the animals in Pig Land, Hyena Land and Learsi, which he willingly shared... saying, "We will be enlisting your aid to help us free the Humans. This freedom mission will be more difficult than what we experienced with you since they are armed not only with nuclear weapons, but high tech weapons like microwave and particle beam weapons, sonic assault weapons and The Death Ray. We may well enlist the help of ET's who are sympathetic with our causes; they have a paralyzing wave generator that will immobilize people without killing them."

Pausing to make sure Farmer John was listening carefully, Enoch continued, "Realize while there are beneficial and helpful ET's you can access, there are just as many who would like nothing better than to also enslave you. In fact, they supported the Pigs and Hyenas and Learsi Elites to install the totalitarian Communist governments under which you most recently suffered! We knew of their relationship with the Pig, Hyena, and Learsi governments and communicated with them before we joined your quest for freedom. We advised them we would be calling in the aid of the ET's with the paralyzing wave generator, oh, and by the way... they also have a matter dissolving ray generator that dissociates the atoms in a body so they no longer can bond or create the molecules that allow a body to remain intact."

Enoch shared even more insights as he disclosed, "Now, you must further develop your psychic abilities as the Natural Land animal nation. We applaud you for using your psychic powers in your campaign to rid yourselves of the Communist menace. Just never grow lazy or complacent. That was your undoing before; not using more discernment about what was being dispensed to you by the Pig Elites and President Ledig. Enjoy your freedom as I just said before, but now in a slightly different way—remain constantly vigilant of schemes from misguided entities that violate Nature and Natural Law. If you need the help of Natural Land, all you have to do is to communicate that need through the inter-dimensional portal we have established between our worlds, and we will be there to aid you. I also have other things to share, but in a slightly different vein."

Farmer John was a little overwhelmed with all that Enoch had shared with him, but felt very indebted to him for all he related. As Enoch continued, he made his points with specific and emphatic arm and hand gestures as he exclaimed, "If you decide to develop your country and start building urban areas, beware of unrestrained development or you will wind up destroying the very thing that supports you... your Mother Earth! An agrarian society is a happy and productive unit of living."

"If you decide to distribute more electricity to your citizens, please remember there are immensely better ways to do this than through fossil fuel electrical generation. There are Tesla electrical energy accumulators, ceramic fuel cells, hydrogen fuel, solar panels and remote solar energy generation that can power vehicles as well as homes. There are even magnetic electrical generators; it is clearly evident the good, non-polluting choices are plentiful and viable!"

As Enoch came to the conclusion of his guidance to Farmer John, he continued with a serious level of wisdom not to be discounted, "Remember too, John, that no governmental structure, even a libertarian government, is necessary when you are guided by Nature and Natural Law. Therein, the Creator distilled equity its template of perfection. Nature's Government is implicit in the Plant and Animal Kingdoms. Nature has no defined constitution yet it operates perfectly and is a form of anarchy, which has been defined as a state of disorder due to absence or non-recognition of authority. Now the naysayers will contend anarchy leads to chaos and bands of roving criminal gangs, but we know in the fractal forms in Nature—where there is no recognized authority—order and perfection exist, and we further know when everyone shares in the bounty of a society and where the hoarding and monopolizing of resources is prohibited, there will be no crime. There will be no roving gangs as needs will have already been met and there will exist no proclivity to criminal activity. Of that, I am certain and most true and you should be too! A government that extracts taxes and fees from its citizens under the color of law and imprisonment to those who do not "pay their fair share," is guilty of de facto extortion and is really just as bad as roving criminal gangs. The difference between them, distilled, is very little if anything!"

The message of wisdom continued as more thoughts surfaced when Enoch, the Elder leader shared from deep in his soul, "Spurn the forlorn ideas the Pig, Hyena and Learsi Elites and cleave to the guidelines of Nature and Natural Law. Live sustainably and you will be much happier, as will your Earth. Be minimalistic in your approach to living... learn from the templates of nature and everything will run smoothly and equitably."

"Remember, within the bounds of governmental entities comes only enslavement. Nature, on the other hand, has no government, either de facto or de jure, and functions more efficiently than any government ever constructed in any animal or human country on Planet Earth!"

Enoch seemed inclined to squeeze as much wisdom as possible into this conversation, and carried on, "I want to reiterate something of utmost critical importance, which is: the naysayers to this foundational belief will demonize it as chaos or anarchy, and you will have roving gangs extorting and taking money from people by force. Is this really any different than what a government does, under the color of law and the constructive extortion you know occurs?"

"If all entities in a country share equally in the bounty of Nature, the problem will be less than touted by those who say governments are a necessary evil! The sardonic nature of this issue is self-evident, since governments are not necessary and have the highest proclivity to degenerate into evil! Let your government be Nature and the Natural Laws there from. The translated law of Nature means share and share alike."

The Laws of Nature also keep you out of the nefarious trap of Commercial/Admiralty Law that infests the third-dimension Human Earth, whereby people are arrested and/or fined for violations of law that hurt nobody and cause damage to nothing. Just as the human Common Law obviates the need for Commercial — and its endless tentacles of control — so does our Natural Law, derived from observing the functioning of Nature, cancel out the need for the odious Commercial Law pitfalls."

"With the "sharing way" of life we summarily eliminate the need for religions organizations. It is really quite simple: God is more powerfully demonstrated and found within God's Cathedral in the wildness of Nature, much more so than any church that has been built or any religion that has been manifested, and Nature is much more useful and enlightened! We all could learn a lot from Yoga and especially Kriya Kundalini Yoga, which is a complete system for living life in a radiant/enlightened manner."

"One last thing, I must share with you," Enoch continued intently, "you need to eliminate the medical system that was created to deal with sickness, since it is economically unsustainable and even more so, unnecessary. Socialized medicine always implodes upon itself because it really has unbearable economic costs. Additionally, it is unnecessary if you are living in a rural society where the energies of Nature, especially the energetic presence of the trees, will keep you naturally healthy, free of sickness and disease and soothing any and all emotional crises; and really, how many emotional crises are you really going to have when you are also surrounded and bathed by a field of negative ions we naturally find in Nature?"

"With that I bid you adieu... but know me and my animals will always be here to consult with! Your success is our success and vice versa."

All Farmer John could do was humbly and gratefully nod his head, up and down in agreement and thank Enoch with a rather primal gratitude. All James and Ann could do, after viewing and hearing such an extended message, was to likewise nod their heads up and down in consonance. Yet the silence between them would not last for long as James was recalling some things very germane to what Enoch had shared

"You know, Ann," James exclaimed, "I recently saw this documentary called "The Next Economy," narrated by Doug Tompkins, about his self sustained communities in Chile and Argentina, and what he shares covers a lot of what Enoch discussed. It shows these events, concepts and experiences in an operational model/template, of how we can continue to live on Earth without destroying ourselves, which is most germane to the human animal."

Upon hearing this, Ann shared her thoughts with James to point out, *This is more your problem than mine, James, because Heaven works much more within the parameters of "Aleph Kaf Aleph, the Seventh Name of God," which I know you understand means perfection or restoring their to their perfect state; but for sure, you can take what works in the higher dimensions of my Heaven and apply to your locale!"*

"Well, Ann," James rejoined, "Doug Tomkins must then have been to Heaven since he has shared how environmentally responsible communities can create the Heaven on Earth you and I were always striving for and which is relevant to the animals of Pig Land, Hyena Land, Learsi and the humans of my Earth subdivision."

"Well, James," communicated Ann, as James centered in on the laughter in her voice, *Doug Tompkins is actually here in Heaven with us now and he is very popular, yet very unassuming, and definitely not "full of himself." He also seems anxious to return to Earth and shepherd the projects he left behind on Planet Earth.*

"I in fact knew that Tompkins made the transition to Heaven, but I did not know you were friends," James responded to Ann. Yet James slowly and with great measure considered his continued response; he really wanted to be accurate in what he next conveyed to her, "Tompkins approach to a sustainable Earth is multi-pronged. As strange as this would sound to many people, us not included Ann, Tompkins talks about beauty as a basic for any economy. Animals might understand this inherently better than humans, but he considers aesthetics... that which is pleasing to the eye... as the cornerstone of the next economy. As artists, both you and I would agree 110%, yet this would probably be beyond the comprehension of most economists, ha-ha!"

"Next," James continued, "Tompkins considers having a water supply in a totally pure state, with zero contamination, as an essential component of the next economy. Now, on an Earth, with an exploding population, potable water sources are becoming scarcer and scarcer, due to various aspects of pollution: industrial, petroleum and natural gas fracking, and mining. And really, Ann, potable water is often a far cry from pure water—so if humanity is to survive, it is one of those "duh" moments that we must immediately stop polluting our Earth, and between animals and humans, the worst polluters are obviously the latter."

"There is another thing about waste I learned from the work of Dr. Gerald Pollack; you might remember him as the University of Washington professor of bioengineering, who developed a theory of water that has been called revolutionary. According to Dr. Pollack, water from deep wells, springs and rivers is much more energetically active, being comprised of

H3O2, which is even better than the H2O2 of Hydrogen Peroxide. Pollack created a company that makes a filter that can create this highly energetic, and very healthful water he calls, EZ Water."

Please continue, James, Ann requested as she intently used her tap into communicating with James. *We both know Mr. Tompkins insights are focused and prescient and it appears Pollack has much to offer, as well!*

"Continue, I will," James volunteered, "since Doug Tompkins discusses how caring for our soils is another fundamental of a green economy, and what we hope is our next economy. Now obviously, glaciated and volcanic soils are going to be highly fertile and agriculturally productive soils, because of their high mineral content. Yet you can take the worst of soils, and through composting, manures, and green manures—the latter being certain legumes and crops that are grown and then plowed into the soil—to create a highly fertile soil. In composting, you can take leaves and pine needles, table scraps, exclusive of meat, and manures, especially of the chicken and horse types, and they will turn into a 'black gold' quality soil enriching amendment. Heck, Ann, you can even take manures, straw, leaves and pine needle and just cover a bad soil with them and it will, over time, create a rich, dark topsoil."

Ann had no time to respond; she sensed James was on a roll. "Now, Ann," James words flowed like the water he spoke of, "Tompkins astutely points out that with no food, there are no people to power an economy. Of course, if said people are Breatharians, they will need very little, if any food, and in fact people might actually feel better without eating, as per Peter Arthur Straubinger's documentary, *In the Beginning There Was Light.*"

"As I understand it, Director P.A. Straubinger completed an arduous ten years of research on the controversial topic of Breatharianism and wrote in a somewhat extensive Director´s Statement, about the scientific and philosophical background of light. He felt there was a need for awareness about its message, address upfront a few possible misunderstandings and provide access to unpublished research material."

"Did you know, Ann, with the advances in science and technology, it has even been proven, scientifically, the human body is capable of taking sunlight and melanin and/or water and creating photosynthesis, which is a process used by plants and other organisms to convert light energy, not to mention phosphorylation, known to turn many protein enzymes on and off, thereby altering their function and activity, in an effort to create energy to live upon—just like what happens with trees and plants? However, we both know, Ann, this is a long way off for most people to even perceive, let alone comprehend, ha-ha, LMAO!"

Ann, seeing a break in James' diatribe, and in agreement with him, allowed her thoughts to surface, *You certainly are the meister of the laugh and laughing, James, but it looks like your ass is still intact, ha-ha... ha-ha!. Please take me to the next plank Doug Tompkins 'platform, ha-ha, touché'!*

"I will do just such, mon amour," James compliantly responded. "Tompkins mentions 'meaningful work' as another part of a sustainable economy. Now, we are not talking about the bizarre corporate culture and jobs therein, that infest Earth, but rather an agrarian economic model. This means, Ann, those people who undertake farming are exalted rather than looked down upon as lowly manual laborers, as has been institutionalized in my Earth dimension. Imagine an Earth where the skilled people who create something from the land and create sustainable structures on the land, are looked up to instead of the attorneys, bankers, stock brokers, doctors and politicians, most of whom are often incapable of making anything with their hands, other than what they can do with their computers!"

I am contemplating that, but the politician part is beyond consideration and you know that, Ann taciturnly replied. *Flipping that flapjack and rewarding those people who can create things in a green manner, as opposed to people who are paper shufflers, or more accurately, making money with the aid of their computers through making trades on the stock market, the commodities exchange and Forex currency exchange, are of an immensely higher value to society, in the short and long run!*

"Yes, I'm in a groove with that, Ann, " James amusingly retorted, "but dig this, as it were, Doug Tompkins also mentions not letting schooling get in the way of your education and knowledge, as was also stated by Mark Twain. So this indicates, Tompkins realizes a school education does not prepare someone to be productive on Earth. My friend and mathematician/numerologist, Lee Douglas Ross, would add to this that all school subjects should be taught in an integrated, cross-disciplinary fashion rather than in accord with the Prussian education system of individual subject education. I learned a lot from him on his website, The Hermetic Way, which I found on the Internet during one of my deep search days at www.t-o-o-l-s.net/."

"Considering more on this subject, who would be more capable of surviving when the shi-ite hits the fan, a highly educated professional person or someone who is handy and can fix and build things and who is knowledgeable and capable in food production?"

Hahahaha, Mr. Smarty Pants." Ann laughingly offered, *"That is really one of your duh moments! Yet you, James of the smart and educated pants, are a Renaissance Man who is capable in both professional and labor based tasks.*

"Indeed, I may be a freak of Nature—or maybe more a student of Nature, Ann," James volunteered, "who is well... let's just say well rounded, as it were, so I can keep moving forward in knowledge like a tree. But let's not digress; more important than my accomplishments... our Mr. Tompkins also mentions the importance of having local energy sources, including those from wind and solar sources. I would add ceramic fuel cells, locally produced hydrogen fuels and magnetic generators as other very viable local energy sources, as well as an energy backup storage provided by the Tesla Industries Battery pack. I would also allude to the BMW and GM vehicles that are fueled by an onboard hydrogen-produced fuel."

Well, James, of the hydrogen fueled smarty pants, Ann responded in a most sardonic fashion, *let's just say sayonara to that nasty, dirty gasoline that infests your planet. You have seen and learned so much and might I mention, the less you pollute your Earth, the more benefitted at the parallel and higher animal and human Earth dimensions and even into the dimensions of Heaven, we all are.*

"Indeed," James loudly proclaimed, "let it be so, Ann, since this greatly lessens our polluting imprint on Planet Earth and in Planet Heaven, hahahaha! While I am amusing myself, I should mention Tompkins' ancillary message of building our structures/housing from both natural and locally obtainable building materials, in a beautiful, esthetic fashion. Conjunct with this, local craftsmen should build these structures, using local traditions. When I saw the documentary showing all of this, it was very clear Tompkins had followed his own advice in his sustainable communities in Chile and Argentina."

For sure, Ann observed, *I know this resonates with you, Mr. Smarty James. I remember Doug sharing with me he felt bio-diversity of animals and plants were most important to him. He mentioned donating huge tracts of land to the Chilean and Argentinean governments to hold in perpetuity as national park preserves. Tompkins also related he created a nursery devoted to the growing of native plants and trees, so as to reforest logged and burned forests and to remediate Earth damage from mining operations.*

"Well, I can see you have been doing your homework, Ann," James replied in awe, "and Tompkins also talks about the raising of animals in a humane and sustainable manner. For me, since I do not eat meat, I would add the production of fish to the mix. So through hatcheries and a symbiotic growing of vegetables and fish through aquaculture, I am super stoked and excited about what we can do in Tomkins view of the next economy, coupled with what I learned and have done myself... and for sure, the Hemp factor should be added to the mix, whether it be for fuel, medicine, clothes or as a hempcrete bio-composite made of the inner woody core of the hemp plant mixed with a lime-based binder used for building structures."

"So anyway, Ann, this is a vision we can replicate— what Tompkins has done and beyond. I feel your sincere need to return to your abode in Heaven, and I guess I need to get back to mine, in kind. I guess I have itchy feet that are in need of a Tweet!"

Smarty and correct about this you are, James of the Hemp pants, Ann agreed with James. *But let us merge our energies in an embrace and kisses, as I miss you so much, and miss being in your presence, even though telepathically we are often linked. Each embrace brings us closer to each other,*

94

leaving a lasting energy imprint upon each other. So sweet it is; do you really have to Tweet?

After their long embrace, the bittersweet reality of Ann's impending departure sank in on James psyche. Keying into his emotions, James realized he was less than thrilled that Ann needed to leave—that their communication was breached, but consoled himself that perhaps the Planet of the Stupids, had become much wiser, and he did too.

Ann subsequently returned to her abode in the high heavens, ascending in an ethereal field of blue and purple and yellow energy, waving goodbye to James as he started the process of pulling himself back to his third-dimension Human Earth, reflecting on the intense turn of events he had witnessed. As a parting message to his beloved Ann, James thoughtfully conjectured, *I guess I do need to get back home and see if I can somehow fix the mess there! Sayonara, my Sweet Ann. Mon Amour.*

Vaya con Dios, Namaste and Hey Resh Chet!

About the Author

Dr. Robert J. Newton has lived his life much in the manner he writes... with a quest to surround himself with the highest level knowledge in the myriad areas that ensure we live rich, full lives. His education has been extensive, ranging from Speech and English at Cal State Fullerton, to a Juris Doctorate from American College of Law, and many certifications in alternative healing. He formalized his career in Naturopathic Medicine as a graduate of Clayton School of Natural Healing.

Newton has lived to serve others; operating an award-winning landscape and design company for many years, as a Christian Science healer for two decades—and more recently as an author, speaker and life and relationship coach. Yoga, Metaphysics, Spiritual Sciences, Natural Healing, World Religions, Ancient Hermetic teachings... this philosopher and champion for the world has tapped into the roots of spirituality, sexuality, life and love—all with the purpose to enlighten those with a common desire to utilize multiple methods and strategies to approach life more effectively, creatively, radiantly and with great abundance.

Today, Dr. Newton lives his life looking forward... honoring the love and the beliefs he shared with his deceased wife, Charlette Newton Smith and writing more novels to plant a "What if" seed in the minds of his readers.

Other Books by the Author

All books by Dr. Newton can be quickly assessed at:

Amazon Author Central:

amazon.com/author/drrobertjnewton

In Search of the Body Immortal:
Let the Journey Begin Paperback -
October 13, 2015

Paperback and Kindle

> Paperback and Kindle
> ASIN: B00VAN8L8Y8
> ISBN-13: 978-0996137140

Beyond the Mists of Time: When Trees
Ruled the Earth And The State of Balance
and Euphoria That Ensued There From

> Paperback and Kindle
> ASIN: B016LGBUW8
> ISBN-13: 978-0996137126

The Hidden Codes of God: A Journey to the Unknown Secrets and Dimensions of the Divine and the Energy of Love

Paperback
ASIN: 0996137106
ISBN-13: 978-0996137102

A Map to Healing and Your Essential Divinity Through Theta Consciousness: Physics of the Immortal "Light Body" and the Creator's Template of Perfection and Abundance for His People!

Paperback
ASIN: 145254445X
ISBN-13: 978-1452544458

Pathways to God: Experiencing the Energies of the Living God in Your Everyday Life

Kindle Edition
ASIN: B00844NSIK

Request for Reader Reviews

Thank you in advance for taking the time to post a review for the book on Amazon; many readers will not take that step to purchase and read... until they know someone else has led the way.

If you enjoyed reading *Planet of the Stupids* I would appreciate it if you would help others enjoy the book, too.

LEND IT. This book is lending enabled, so please feel free to share with a friend.

RECOMMEND IT. Please help other readers find the book by recommending it to readers' groups, discussion boards, Goodreads, etc.

REVIEW IT. Please tell others why you liked this book by reviewing it on the site where you purchased it, on your favorite book site, or your own blog.

EMAIL ME. I'd love to hear from you.

theta4ia@yahoo.com

http://www.drrobertnewton.com/

www.ingramcontent.com/pod-product-compliance
Lightning Source LLC
Chambersburg PA
CBHW060429260626
47161CB00005B/1844